Tales of Woe

As Well As Other Preposterous but Humorous Events

Copyright 2008 by J. Francis Angier

Published by **J. Francis Angier**

Printed by **Blanchard Litho**
3 Conley Street
Sherbrooke, Quebec J1M 1L8
Canada

Edited by **The Little House Desktop Publishing**
West Glover, VT 05875

First Edition

D0095669

ISBN: 978-0-615-22994-2

Written by
J. Francis Angier
7 Chelsea Place
Williston Vermont 05495-9479
802-879-7215
francisangier@comcast.net

DEDICATION

This book is dedicated to my aunt and uncle,
Byron and Emma Angier Clark.

My aunt and uncle who brought me up in New Haven, Vermont September 1944

This wonderful couple took me in for a few weeks when I was four years old because my mother was very ill. My mother never recovered and spent the rest of her life an invalid so my stay at the Clarks stretched out to fourteen years, providing me with an upbringing that has benefited me for a lifetime. A little history of their lives is needed to understand their character and the positive effect they had on many people.

Byron Clark (1878–1953) managed to buy a farm on the "River Road" near New Haven Mills, Vermont, about 1905. He worked very hard improving the farm and paid off the mortgage in twelve years. He married Emma Angier (1884–1963) in 1907 and together they built a modest farm business producing milk, firewood, timber and livestock. They lived frugally but comfortably and bought their first car, a 1915 Model T Ford that they used for business and for visiting family and friends. My Aunt Emma kept a daily diary for 56 years recording their activities: how many quarts of produce they canned, sold or gave away; national events such as elections, the sinking of the Titanic, World War I, the Depression, great floods and storms; as well as those who came to visit; births, deaths and illnesses are also there for me to look up as all the diaries are in my possession.

After selling their first farm they never owed debts to anyone and never bought anything unless they had the money to pay for it. After moving to the farm where I was brought up they helped many people of all ages. Several people lived their last years with them in comfort and safety, while a number of young students boarded with them while attending the local high school. During the Depression, family members came for the weekends, enjoyed great meals, and went home with canned goods or a bag of potatoes to supplement their meager fare in those tough times. They were truly a generous couple.

My uncle maintained strict discipline, was very punctual, did not drink or smoke and never used foul language, nor did anyone else under his roof. They had no children of their own but nurtured and influenced many young people, always setting proper if somewhat stringent rules and examples. My aunt filled her role as a super cook and maintained a comfortable and tidy house. I worked very hard from the age of five with duties commensurate with my age, size and strength—by the time I became a teenager my uncle and I functioned as a team.

All the good examples I grew up with did not rub off on me but the memories of my life on the farm with those two remarkable people never leave me for a single day. This collection of corny stories does not relate closely to them but they would both chuckle over some of them, and so this little story of their life together fits in as a life well lived and very well remembered.

ACKNOWLEDGMENTS

The stories in this book are not one percent of the events that crowd my memory but many of these tales would not have appeared had it not been for our five sons. Their curiosity, their questions, their spontaneous remarks and capers as they grew up on the farm brought me great joy and amusement. Because of interest in my younger years they drew stories from me of events that had been dormant and considered by me to be of no interest to growing boys. Now that they are all more than forty five years old and I am forty years older than the youngest it is pleasant to reflect on those wonderful years when they were so inquisitive and full of humor.

John, our oldest, asked me where the road past our house went and thinking it was safe to tell a three year old that he could go anywhere he wanted to on that road I never guessed he would try to go everywhere during his life. He became a stock broker, salesman and a pilot. I owe Michael because he asked so many questions about everything that I didn't have answers to. He and his wife, Dawn, have a world-wide motivational business. They relax on "Attitude" a nice sailboat. Phillip was the most reticent of them all and was the least mischievous but apparently that was because he must have been planning to be a good business man early on and he has succeeded as a builder. He and his wife, Debbie, have a nice home and a large modern powerboat. Pierre was a worker and wanted to do everyting. By nine years old he had decided to become a Doctor and he became an exceptinally good one. Now he has sold his practice, "Get Well" and he and his wife, Colleen, are traveling in their RV while he decides what to do next. Now we come to the "French Leprechaun" Thomas Patrick Angier who early on had a terrific sense of humor and a fantastic memory. He has always been interested and knowledgeable about almost everyting. He knows a great deal about the environment, plants, animals, birds, science and is also a builder specializing mostly in tile.

All of them love Vermont and Lake Champlain and all have had boats but rarely have I ever found brothers so intensely interested in so many diverse aspects of the world and all that is in it. So this has enabled me to derive inspiration for writing about many issues and I must admit that they as well, write and are much more articulate than I am. With over a half dozen books published and the potential for many more on the way, our sons will continue to bring pleasure and appreciation to their parents. Madeleine, the mother of these five sons and my wife for the past sixty one years deserves the most credit for any and all successes our family has enjoyed.

Sept, 2006
From left to right
John Jr, Michael, Phillip, Pierre and Thomas

FOREWORD

For as far back as I can remember my father has always had a story to tell. You can tell one is coming by the sparkle in the corner of his eye. This usually will happen in the course of conversation, and like a dog waiting obediently for a bone—all the while about to bust at the seams in anticipation—he waits for the person to finish speaking.

Then he enthusiastically begins his story, some short and cute, others excruciatingly long—some of eloquent wit, others downright corny, but always appropriate to the situation.

That is the true art of humor, to recall a tale that fits the moment. Anybody can tell a joke, but to tell one at the right time, and with the proper flavor, "Ah, that is the rub."

As you read these words of woe and wit, be advised some are accurate to the letter; however, some are slightly embellished, some to the point of extreme, but all well told.

These stories are a stark contrast to his previous book, *Ready or Not: Into the Wild Blue,* that chronicled the many hardships he has endured in his life. But in many ways complements it, for it is humor that has enabled him to endure the many adversities and made the rainbows of life more colorful.

That book, unlike this one, was in no need of any embellishment. It is a fascinating story unto itself. And without a doubt; the greatest story he has ever told.

Enjoy these tales of a lifetime. I have and always will. Reading them is "funner'n hell."

Thomas Patrick Angier

INTRODUCTION

Many readers may have heard some of these stories before while others may not be so familiar with them. Some are original for this collection and some are based on actual happenings, usually slightly enhanced. Most are humorous; a few are, as the title suggests, about somewhat sad events; others are personal but factual. Hopefully, most will be entertaining and perhaps nostalgic to a few older readers. Humor has been a crutch for me to help block out hauntingly painful memories of my past as a prisoner of war during World War II in Germany and Poland. My personal knowledge of the atrocities that took place in the Nazi death camps around us has been the hardest to erase. Humor has often helped to take the edge off.

It is my hope that a little levity from these stories will brighten your days just as it has mine over the years.

J. Francis Angier

Tales of Woe

As Well as Other Preposterous but Humorous Events

Skilled Plow Person

While traveling through southwestern England my wife and I noticed some plowing had been started on a very steep hillside meadow. My curiosity was aroused because in my many years of farming I had never seen tillage attempted on such a steep slope, even in the hilliest parts of Vermont. It just didn't seem possible a tractor could be negotiated in that field and certainly horses would not be able to be driven up there, especially hitched to any kind of plow. Pulling over to the side of the narrow road I studied the scene for a time and concluded the only possible solution was to drive a tractor up a less steep approach to one side of the piece of land and carefully proceed to the work area along the ridge. The furrows had all been plowed *down* the slope but to me it seemed it would be a terrifying ordeal to start down that steep hill even with the plows engaged to provide some braking effect.

Observing a driveway leading to a farmstead we drove into the yard and saw a shiny new Massy Ferguson tractor with matching plows attached. Striking up a conversation with the man polishing the hood of the tractor, we learned he was the owner of the farm and obviously the new tractor as well. The farmer explained the field would be seeded down to pasture grass and harvested by his sheep and cattle as no harvesting equipment could be risked on the steep slope. I inquired how the seeding would be accomplished and he answered, "Oh, the seed has to be scattered by hand, a fairly tedious operation but of course it isn't necessary to go through this procedure very often. It may well be 10 or 20 years before the field needs working up again."

I observed, "It appears to be quite dangerous to plow down such a precipitous slope."

"Yes, it does take a bit of courage and skill." The man seemed to be fidgeting quite a bit for an Englishman and we noticed he frequently glanced towards the house so I thought perhaps we were holding him up from his work. His wife may have preferred he get going rather than idly chatting with tourists. Just as I was about to apologize for holding him up his wife came striding out dressed in a warm sweater, work trousers and boots. With only a nod to us she swung her leg up over the tractor seat and quickly started the Ferguson. She lifted the hydraulic plows up to transport position, put the machine in gear and began to drive out of the yard. Her husband called after her, "Mind my Fergie, Love!"

We left almost immediately as the farmer seemed a bit embarrassed but I pulled to one side of the road to watch the operation. Sure enough, we saw the red "Fergie" making its way across the top of the field and then the plows were carefully lowered and the woman guided the tractor slowly down the steep slope. The plows neatly turned the black soil over adding another two furrows to the completed work. Once safely down, the skilled plow person started back up the safer, less steep, edge of the field to repeat the process. Finally, I could start breathing again. If there were a near vertical field like that on my farm I wouldn't plow it nor would I send *my wife* up there to do it even with a shiny new "Fergie."

Baby's First Visit to the Doctor

A woman and a baby were in the doctor's office for the infant's first examination. The doctor examined the baby with the usual occasional "Hummm." Finally he asked if the baby was "bottle fed" or "breast fed." When the woman answered "breast fed," the doctor told her to strip to the waist and he made a thorough examination of her breasts. He squeezed her nipples and gave her breasts a lengthy handling, then looked at her closely and said, "No wonder this baby is underweight. You have no milk!"

"Of course not," the woman said smiling. "I'm his grandmother but I'm glad I came."

Muscle Man

Thomas Williams decided to do some muscle building after several years of sedentary living and working at a desk job. The first week he started lifting two five-pound potato sacks holding them out at arm's length for a count of ten. The second week he moved up to ten-pound potato sacks and, feeling quite proud of his progress, he began the third week by putting potatoes into the sacks.

Whoomp!

My younger brother married a delightful Georgia girl who had never been north into Yankee country until he brought her up for a visit. She had an idea that we had to be kissing cousins to Eskimos to live in such a cold part of the country. Finally, she asked in her endearing southern drawl, "How do you all tolerate those severe winters?" Seizing the moment, I decided to impress her with what it took to cope with the rigors of a Vermont winter. "My Dear, you can scarcely imagine how bitter cold it gets here. Why, I've seen it so far below zero we had to wait several minutes after someone said something to hear what it was they were talking about. And *snow*! It isn't too bad unless we get a four-foot snowfall and when four feet of snow come down onto you with a great big *Whoomp*, you know you are in Vermont!"

That analogy didn't backfire until some time later because my brother never said a word. He just walked out for a good laughing jag where she couldn't hear him. Some months later back in Georgia some one straightened out my sister-in-law so for about the next three years she scarcely spoke a word to me. Just an example of how hard it is to make a joke when you have an honest face! People tend to believe anything you say.

The Georgia girl did get her revenge. When our oldest son, John, accompanied me on a trip to Notre Dame for a Charismatic Conference, we stopped at my brother's place, at that time, in Cleveland, Ohio, and my gracious sister-in-law invited us to stay overnight. Our sleeping area was on a lower level from the living room and when I awoke in the morning I was shocked to see a huge Confederate flag draped over the railing at the head of my bed. So if you have an honest face, don't tell such a preposterous tale to a young, curious and trusting girl from the South—or possibly from other parts of the world as well.

A Failure to Communicate

Many years ago I hired a fifteen-year-old "reform school" boy to help me for a few days. He was an unfortunate member of a dysfunctional family and was sent to the school not because he was troublesome but because his family didn't want him. This happened too often in those times so while he was with us I tried to teach him about things that would make his life better, as well as show him how a bit of humor can often take the edge off at times. He was a little slow mentally but honest and he really tried to do well as he helped me with the haying.

One afternoon I could see he was getting tired so while I finished baling a small field of hay near our house I told him to just take it easy. He stood by my tractor and asked, "But what do you want me to do?" I told him, "Hold down that bale of hay while I finish tying up this field." Poor choice of terminology. It was my way of telling him to sit down on the bale of hay and rest but when I came around the field again he was firmly holding down the bale with a pitchfork. I told him he had held it down long enough so now he could sit on it and watch the cars go by. A half hour later when the field was all baled he came over to report he had counted eleven cars.

There were other little incidents that struck me as rather funny but I always tried to not embarrass him. We ran out of gasoline on a lower meadow so I asked him to get a five-gallon can from our garage, take it to the store and bring me back five gallons of gasoline. It was less than half a mile to the store but a good lug for a kid to carry it back down to the field, which he did cheerfully. As I was pouring it into the tank I realized it was kerosene not gasoline. Of course this necessitated draining the tank and making another trip but although he was very sorry, almost in tears, we passed it off as a humorous event.

We often wondered what became of him and hoped our treatment of him helped in some small way. We lost track of him but surmised he just melted into our great country and probably he himself told someone to hold down something by sitting on it.

Disposal

When I was five and six years old one of my many chores was to take the potato peelings from the kitchen down to feed to the bull. My route to the monster's stall was out through the summer kitchen, through a long corridor of a building that connected the house to the barn, down a stairway to the ground floor of the barn and finally a 110-foot walk to the bull's stall at the far end of the barn.

He was a fierce looking beast with large wild eyes and an ominous bellow when anyone approached him. It was a terrifying journey for me and the closer I came the slower I walked. The feed manger had a high front so it was necessary for a little guy like me to raise the big pan (we used a lot of potatoes in our household) up above my head and dump it into the manger. The bull would roar loudly and immediately start eating the peelings but it didn't sound like he was grateful— more as if he was annoyed to have his food delivered by a little pipsqueak. I would run away as fast as I could hoping there was no way he could get loose and chase me.

After a time, it occurred to me that if the peelings were dumped into the space under the stairs it would avoid my having to face that big creature. He would bellow loudly as if he knew I was cheating him of his treat. After a week or two the peelings apparently gave off an odor because my uncle investigated the dark, trash-filled area under the stairs with a flashlight. He had noticed a few peelings on the top of the partition that partially enclosed the space under the stairs. He led me to the site and asked if that was my doing and once that fact was verified he ordered me into the dark hole to get every last peeling from among all the old wire, useless tin pails and assorted junk on the dusty floor of the area. I knew it was often frequented by large rats that even the barn cats never dared to follow. It was a very obnoxious assignment but somehow after that ordeal the bull didn't seem quite as formidable and it was one of many lessons taught me while growing up—to always carry out instructions.

Getting the Bull Home

Two sisters, Candy and Cindy, inherited the family ranch. Candy didn't care for school so she had very little education while her sister took business courses and graduated from college. Even so, in just a few years, they were in financial trouble.

In order to keep the bank from repossessing the ranch Cindy decided they needed to purchase a bull located quite a way off to breed their own stock but they had only $600 left. Before leaving to buy the bull Cindy told her sister, "After I buy the bull, I will contact you to drive out there and haul it home."

Cindy decided to buy the bull but she had to pay $599 for it. After paying the stockyard man she drove into town to send a telegram to Candy. She walked into the telegraph office and said, "I want to send a telegram to my sister telling her to hitch the trailer to our pickup and come after a bull I've bought." The telegraph operator told her it would cost 99 cents a word. Realizing she had only $1 left she decided to send one word. "I want you to send her the word 'comfortable.'"

The operator shook his head. "How will your sister ever know what you want her to do if you send just the word 'comfortable'?" Cindy explained, "My sister never went to school much so she will read it very slowly—'com-for-da-bul.'"

Not on Monday

A couple had been married a few years and decided to get a divorce although they appeared to get along very well. They discussed it at length but could not resolve their differences and agreed to try once more by seeing a marriage counselor. After listening to them for a time the counselor told the husband, "This woman needs a lot of attention." Then to emphasize his point he grabbed the attractive girl, wrapped his arms around her and kissed her several times. "Now that is just what she needs and I want her to get this kind of treatment at least every Monday, Wednesday and Friday." The young man seemed to agree. "OK, I can bring her in Wednesdays and Fridays but I bowl on Mondays."

You Had Better Get Up!

"Paul! Get up right now and get dressed or you will be late for school." Paul rolled over and started to snooze again. His mother shouted up the stairway again. "Paul, get up this minute, there is no time to spare. Do you hear me?"

"I don't want to go to school, I hate school, I hate the kids, the teachers, even the janitor," moaned Paul.

His mother gave it her best shot. "Paul, you are forty-two years old and you are the principal so get going or I will call the truant officer!"

Think About It

Tom's first job didn't pay very well so after several months he got up nerve enough to ask his boss for a raise.

"Why can't you pay me what I'm worth?" blurted Tom.

"I would gladly, my boy, but how would you live on it?"

Lucky Guy

A young man from the city, Ike worked for me one busy spring planting time and did very well as a tractor driver after a bit of training. We were working on fields that were a few miles from the house so my wife put up lunches for us in a sturdy paper bag that I stashed on a huge boulder on a corner of the field we were working on. Ike was always close by on his tractor so I could observe his work. He had asked permission to let his faithful dog go along with us to romp over the fields and some nearby woods.

One day I played a trick on him at our noon break. I shut down my tractor near the boulder and motioned to Ike to do the same but by the time he joined me I was eating my sandwich and tried to have a sympathetic look on my face. "Ike, your dog got into our lunch and wouldn't you know he ate *your* sandwich," I lied.

Ike was honest and agreeable but because of his upbringing he lacked any sense of humor. Without slowing down, he turned around and started back to his machine apparently willing to forego lunch and believing his dog had somehow chosen *his* sandwich. Of course I called him back and told him it was just a joke and not only would he have his lunch but a tasty morsel had been included for his dog. During the few weeks he worked for me he began to develop a liking for funny things like that.

On his last day I sent him out alone to mow a field of hay. "Just open the gate on the right side of the road and cut the hay on that nice level field." A few hours later as I went to check on his work I met him on his way home.

"That field sure has a lot of stumps in it," he said.

"What? There isn't a stump or obstacle in that whole field," I shouted.

"You did tell me to cut the field on the left side of the road didn't you?" he said in a panic-stricken voice.

"No! No!" I yelled. "The field on the left belongs to my neighbor. You cut his prize seed field!"

Ike nearly fell off his tractor laughing because he had finally played a trick on me. He had cut the hay in the right field, done a professional job of it and dreamed up that joke to play on me. A little humor had rubbed off on Ike and I hoped he cultivated it as he went through life.

Another Way of Putting It

A somewhat overweight girl in my class was often joked about and shunned by her classmates and this annoyed me enough to counsel some of the other students with very little effect. I made it a point to always say good morning to her and occasionally have a little conversation although I was quite shy around all girls. One day she brought up the fact that most of the attention she received was from me and she told me how much she appreciated that. "It doesn't seem to bother you that I'm fat," she said. "Well, my dear, I would never call you fat. Let's just say you have a generous figure." By golly, that was almost seventy years ago and that observation still makes points for me with a lot of ladies who have "generous figures."

April Fools' Day

Approaching Chattanooga, Tennessee, on our way home from Florida we decided to have our motor home washed at a really nice facility. It was more convenient to unhook our tow car and the very congenial crew took care of that and even washed the car for free as well. I kidded them as I prepared to drive away. "I hope you remembered to tie our car back on." They played along by pretending they had indeed neglected to hook us up again and even told me they couldn't find our vehicle and probably someone had driven off with it. We were not able to observe the tow car unless we were making a turn but Madeleine had walked to the rear window and checked to be sure it was secured and ready to roll.

Right away I had an idea because it was April 1st. We called our sons and said we had made a big faux pas. We had driven away from a car wash and forgotten to hitch up our car and were looking for an exit to turn around and drive 30 miles back to retrieve it. They laughed up a storm at our "senior moment" and believed us, not realizing it was April Fools' Day.

My worst prank for April Fools' Day was bittersweet. Dear friends of ours had promised to come to Vermont to visit us for several seasons but it didn't work out. Finally, they solemnly promised to come the next summer. To show my skepticism I even asked what color their car was so I could watch for it coming up our driveway. On April 1st I called and asked what they were doing at the moment. The dear lady answered, "Just relaxing and watching TV, but what are you doing and where are you calling from?" I answered casually, "We are halfway between Wickenburg and Kingman." They lived in Kingman, Arizona, at the time so she panicked because theoretically, we would have been less than an hour away. She tossed the phone to her husband shouting we were coming to see them right away. She dashed upstairs and started tearing the spare bed up to put on new linens and all.

Before I could tell her husband it was a joke and we were still in Vermont he began to tell me how delighted they were to have us visit them and could we stay longer this time. By the time I convinced him it was all a big joke he laughed and said he had never seen his wife run upstairs so fast. By the time she got the message she had put the spare room in first class order but they both shared the trick I had played on them with a great deal of amusement.

It still grieves me to recall that episode because although we all laughed about it at the time we received tragic news soon after. They were both killed in a terrible auto accident when they were struck head on by a drunken driver. They were a wonderful couple. He was a classmate of mine and a delight to spend time with. We had kept in close touch for many years and managed to visit each other whenever our travels allowed it. That was one of my tricks that I regret.

When I was six years old and not into tricks myself, I spoiled my aunt's April Fools' joke. A half-dozen men came to our place to saw up our next winter's supply of firewood and it was exciting for me to observe the men lifting the big logs onto a saw to be cut into short pieces as long as I stayed a distance away from the dangerous machine.

On a quick trip to the kitchen before lunch I managed to sneak a few delicious hot cookies from the table. Whenever the sawing crew came around to the various farms in the area they were treated to the best meals the ladies could come up with. Stuffing a cookie into my mouth as I watched the men shut down for lunch, I found a piece of cloth baked into the cookie. The men watched me pull out the cloth and do the same with a second cookie. During the meal the men all refused the cookies much to my aunt's dismay. I had sabotaged her April Fools' joke.

Deer Camp/Dear Camp

The four great deer slayers of the village always looked forward to their sojourn at the camp they had built and furnished high up in a wooded area. They purchased a few acres from the farmer who lived at the access road to the property and paid him well to keep the gate locked during deer hunting season. In the autumn of 1957, the four arrived at the farm with huge amounts of food, booze and even remembered to bring weapons and hunting knives. After admonishing the old farmer to keep the gate locked they drove their four-wheel drive vehicles over the steep winding road to their base of operations.

Shortly after settling in it began to rain—a light, cold drizzle along with fog that restricted vision enough to prevent safe hunting. This was not a great impediment to enjoying the two-week stay with a roaring fire going and plenty of nourishing food and drink. The rain persisted for days but that didn't dampen spirits.

The four wives were enjoying the interlude as well with card parties, shopping sprees and just plain celebrating not having the four spouses underfoot. By the end of the first week the women realized the continuing wet weather must be quite boring for the hunters. They decided to bake up a storm, make delicious hot dishes and take it up to the men, imagining they would relish a few home-cooked meals.

With considerable hilarity and anticipating a romantic weekend with their menfolk, the four laughing, joking women drove out to the remote countryside to bring relief to the men "roughing it" in the dreary woods. After all those cold meals and boring days shut up in the primitive cabin, the wives would be looked upon as angels of mercy. "How thoughtful of us" they were thinking as they pulled up to the gate across the access road.

The old farmer came rushing out of the house but instead of unlocking the gate he pushed his head and shoulders into the station wagon as soon as they rolled the window down. "Ladies, ladies, you can't go up there. They've brought their wives with them this year!"

Neighborhood Revolving Chicken Dinners

In the small New England town of Spencer, the citizens prided themselves on maintaining an extremely low crime rate and were able to solve most of the infringements through their own local authorities. The Town Constable and the Poor Master kept a close watch on everyone. Newcomers to the area were investigated by Tom Hallock, the Overseer of the Poor, not only to see that needy persons had a place to stay and food to eat, but also if they intended to remain any length of time. The newcomers had to find work so as not to become a burden to the taxpayers or they were sent on their way. Fred Paine, the constable, watched for any suspicious activities and reported to the selectmen who were empowered to hold a trial to resolve any problem. No one could remember a time when the County Sheriff or State Police had to be called in. The town of Spencer took care of its own.

There had always been a bizarre system of tolerance among the citizens in regard to missing chickens. If a family discovered a hen, or even two or three birds unaccounted for, they didn't raise a ruckus because very soon they would be invited to a chicken dinner, usually by a neighbor. These quite frequent social get-togethers helped make for a tight community.

In October of 1929, the Perkins family was shocked to discover six of their high- producing Rhode Island Red hens were missing, resulting in six fewer eggs every day. With no large gathering of chicken pie connoisseurs taking place for the next three days, the Perkins called the constable. Word spread quickly and it appeared a major theft had occurred and a serious breach of etiquette had struck the community. Suspicion centered upon Sean Muldoon, the only Catholic among the solid Congregationalists and an Irishman as well. The Red Front Store where everyone did their trading, reported Sean, had six more eggs than usual to exchange for groceries. A visit by Constable Fred Paine heightened the suspicion when he observed Sean's henhouse seemed somewhat overcrowded.

Muldoon was a loner who worked at odd jobs and was very skilled at repairing whatever was broken. He was frequently on call for snowplowing, shoveling driveways, splitting wood, helping to butcher, or almost anything people needed help with. He was a World War I veteran but rarely spoke of it, although men who had served with him in France regarded him as a hero.

The Town Fathers decided to hold a trial for Muldoon after he was formally charged with theft. The game plan, as usual, was to have the moderator of the town meetings (held every first Tuesday of March) to be the judge, the three selectmen would serve as jurors and the townspeople would, of course, observe. Harvey Hewitt, a close friend of Muldoon, would act as his attorney. Harvey was well-suited to the task as he was extremely articulate and sharp-witted. He told Muldoon he would take the case providing he (Hewitt) could do all the talking. There was a reason Harvey wanted his client to remain silent, perhaps because the veteran of The Great War had reputedly had more than a whiff of poison gas that left him, mentally, running on three cylinders at times.

The moderator took his place on a raised platform at the back of the town hall behind a podium, armed with his ancient gavel handed down to him by his father, who inherited it from his father. Harvey held forth from the space in front of the podium between the three selectmen and his client, Muldoon, while the crowd occupied the main part of the hall. The middle selectman, Mark Peters, was hard of hearing and intensely interested in the proceedings so he leaned as far forward as possible in his rickety armchair.

Harvey prosecuted his case aggressively as if the fate of the nation rested on his efforts. First he focused on the circumstantial evidence presented by the constable, calling into question the accuracy of the accusations against his client. Then he came to his starring role, presenting Muldoon as an impeccable, upstanding, righteous citizen, an indispensable pillar of the community. In a lowered voice, Harvey caught the full attention of everyone. In the silence the audience achieved in order to hear Harvey's words, one could have heard a pin drop. The emotional atmosphere his praise for the accused generated brought tears to the eyes of one elderly lady. When Harvey's voice began to rise to a crescendo, there were a few sobs from the back of the room. An almost inaudible whimper escaped from Mark Peters who had stretched his long scrawny neck towards the drama taking place on the floor. Harvey held his arm out straight towards his client causing him to shrink back in his chair as he drove home the fact that a man of Muldoon's character could never stoop so low as to steal a neighbor's chickens. Then as he swung his arm around suddenly while shouting that a poor innocent man had been wrongly accused, his forefinger grazed Mark Peter's nose. The old man let out a screech and dodged back so suddenly he tipped his chair over backwards but the other two selectmen, one each side, managed to catch the arms of the chair in time to prevent it from going completely over.

As this bit of activity subsided, the moderator rose and whacked his gavel for silence stopping Harvey in mid-sentence. "We have heard enough! This exemplary man could not have committed this crime. Mr. Muldoon, you are completely exonerated." Amidst the turmoil Muldoon rose and attempted to speak but Harvey clapped a hand over his mouth and wrestled him towards the door. However, Muldoon managed to escape momentarily and shouted, "Judge! Judge! You said I'm completely X-ON-OR-ATED. Does that mean I get to keep the chickens?!!!"

Transition

A Vermont man had a nice farm on the banks of the Connecticut River but the 1927 flood caused the river to cut in back of the farm so the owner woke up in New Hampshire. People wondered how he felt about becoming an instant citizen of New Hampshire. "I'm happy and relieved. There's no way I could stand another Vermont winter!" he replied.

Cold!

One day up in Newport, Vermont, it was so cold I saw a politician with his hands in his own pockets!

Vermonters

Henry and Edna lived up in the hills on a hardscrabble farm outside of Chelsea almost in the geographical center of Vermont. A bachelor friend, Earl, frequently stopped by for a good meal and a chat.

One afternoon as he and Henry sat on the porch reminiscing, Earl kept glancing through the screen door at Edna and finally made some comments. "That woman of yours is sure a good cook, all-round housekeeper and damned good looking for a gal her age. Yes sir, she's one in a million and you sure are lucky to have her. She's right nice to look at, and it must be a pleasure to be married to a woman like Edna." "Ayah," drawled Henry. "She be all those things and more. Sometimes it's almost more than I can stand not to tell her so."

Henry and Edna finally lucked out and sold their farm to some flatlander city folk for enough money to retire in Florida. Edna loved St. Petersburg but Henry was bored. Their relationship was somewhat strained. One evening, Edna remarked, "Henry, do you know what day this is?"

"I guess it's Saturday," he answered.

"Well it's our forty-fifth anniversary and you ought to be ashamed of yourself for not remembering," she admonished.

"Is that so?" replied Henry.

"You know we should talk because one of these days one of us will be gone," continued Edna.

Henry picked up his newspaper again and responded, "Ayah, you are right about that, and when it happens I'm moving back to Chelsea!"

The Road Builder

Rolf Patterson had been the town road commissioner for nearly thirty years but finally felt too old to continue struggling to maintain the crooked, hilly roads in his central Vermont town. Freshets washed out culverts and roadbeds, while in winter, equipment became stalled in huge snowbanks. When he saw an advertisement for bids to build a road out West he responded and was delighted to hear his bid was accepted.

Arriving at the site he stared at the level landscape with no hills in sight and felt his dreams of easy road work had come true. The plans called for a perfectly straight road with not a single curve with not much need for many culverts. Rolf assembled a small crew and began his project, employing his usual frugal methods. The work progressed rapidly and was completed in a few short weeks. Finally he called the inspectors to check out his work so he could collect his compensation and pay the bills he had incurred.

He was astounded to hear the lengthy criticism of his work by the officials, as the road looked like a beautiful piece of engineering. But they complained the road was too narrow, the macadam too thin, the shoulders not wide enough and the culverts inadequate for flash flooding. The inspectors suddenly stopped and stared incredulously into the distance. It appeared Rolf had been too ecstatic over the ease of road building on the perfectly level land compared to the mountainous roads he had struggled with for so many years. He had overdone the project. His new road stretched twenty-two miles beyond the state line. He addressed the fussy inspectors, "You fellers found fault with every part of my construction—the width, the thickness of material, the culverts, but not a word about its most outstanding feature. So tell me, how is it for length?"

Really?

A small country store kept the usual variety of goods from hardware to canned goods and other nonperishable items. Because it was within walking distance from our home we frequently stopped in for small purchases and of course always heard a bit of gossip from the two old proprietors, Fred and Amos. For years they stocked my favorite cereal so one morning I hurried down to get a box as we had none of that special cereal left for breakfast. It was shocking to learn they had none, and would not be ordering any more. Even more surprising was their reason for discontinuing my favorite cereal. "It sells too fast. We are always running out of it." Could be I had praised it too often to other customers.

Another eccentricity the two old bachelor brothers shared was a propensity for avoiding family members. A dear friend of mine with a terrific Irish sense of humor felt badly that the large family never got together nor did they communicate in any way with each other. He dreamed up a scheme to bring them together and decided the quicker the better as they were all getting up in years. One of the bachelors, Fred, was rumored to have stashed away a bit of money and in those times (the 1930s), several thousand dollars was enough to cause people, especially relatives, to wonder what would become of the money when the old man died.

My friend Pat who had known the family for many years was on very good terms with the two storekeepers and often joked about their idiosyncrasies. Amos kept a flock of chickens so they ate lots of eggs and had frequent chicken dinners. He also went out to pump gas for the occasional customer while Fred watched the cash register and sat most of the time by the door in his rocker petting a big gray cat.

Pat set the stage for the great reunion to bring most of the family members to the store. He started the rumor one day all over town that Fred had died so word spread rapidly to all the family. About seven o'clock that evening, brother Ambrose and his wife entered the store all dressed up. They were somewhat startled to see Fred rocking away but took the chairs Amos brought out for them although no one had spoken a word. A few minutes later cousin Jean arrived, also in a dark suit that smelled of mothballs. Amos brought out another chair. Two other brothers and their wives walked soberly into the store followed by sisters Marie and Celine. Another cousin and the youngest brother, Andrew, finally exhausted the supply of chairs. Fred had sat rocking in his chair stroking the old cat with his heavy brown cap pulled down over his forehead as usual. While the well-dressed family sat quietly, Amos stood in the middle of the room with his hands deep in his pockets glancing from one to the other completely bewildered. Finally, old Fred yelled out, "What the hell is going on here?" Pat had been listening and observing the comings and goings from the large front porch of the store. When Fred spoke up, Pat was laughing so hard he was rolling on the floor and a few bystanders who had come to see the show began to cheer. Pat had brought the large French family together at last.

Another Earful?

Two younger farmers lived about two miles apart and to each other's benefit often worked together and exchanged any information that might help their farms be more profitable. They shared equipment to reduce overhead and when extra help might be needed they just helped each other instead of spending money for outside labor. It was a wonderful and close relationship that proved to be profitable. They set aside a half hour or so each evening to make plans, exchange ideas and discuss the latest innovations in agriculture by telephone.

There was one flaw in this communication system—they were on a "party line." They were both aware that neighbors listened in occasionally and one lonely widow never missed any of their conversations. This did not deter the young men from having their evening chats. One evening as they concluded an interesting and somewhat controversial talk, embellished to impress the widow, of course, they played a little trick on the delightful but curious lady.

"Well, goodnight, my friend," said Alan.
"Goodnight, old buddy," replied Dave." Then in the next second Dave spoke quietly, "Good night, Mrs. Eddy." And immediately came the reply, "Goodnight, Dave."

The Hero

Up in the Northeast Kingdom of Vermont there were occasional house fires often caused by overheated wood stoves or a spark flying out onto the floor. One very cold day a man saw his neighbor's house on fire and rushed over to see how he could help. There were no other homes on the dead-end road and it was nearly fifteen miles to the nearest fire station so there was no way to put out the fire as the building was engulfed in flames. The owner was a heavy-set woman with three children, two of whom were at school. The woman was outside with her elderly mother but the third child, a boy about five years old had been sleeping upstairs and the two women had not been able to reach him as the stairwell was a mass of flame and the second floor was filled with dense smoke.

Sizing up the situation, the neighbor pulled a ladder from a shed and seizing an ax climbed up to a window. When he smashed the window to gain access the smoke poured out but by putting his heavy overcoat over his head the man entered the room and finally located the little boy unconscious on the floor. He was nearly overcome himself by the thick smoke but managed to carry the boy down the ladder, bundled him into his car and with the hysterical distraught women wailing in the back seat, he rushed over the snow-covered roads to the nearest doctor. After making arrangements for the trio to stay with relatives, he drove home past the totally destroyed house and went to bed as the smoke had made him quite ill.

The next morning he wondered how the little boy he had rescued was doing as the boy had incurred some serious burns, but he had no phone to call anyone. At about noon someone brought the mother to his house and in anticipation of hearing how the boy was doing he rushed out into the yard to greet the woman. She stood solidly with both feet on the ground, with her hands deep in the pockets of her parka, looked him in the eye and spoke. "You wouldn't know what become of his leather jacket while you were up in his room, would you?"

Singing Telegram

Susan Van Dusan had always wanted to receive a telegram so when Western Union called to say she had one and they were calling to be sure someone would be there to receive it, she became very excited. "Oh, please send it as a singing telegram!" she pleaded. The caller told her it might be inappropriate and didn't have anyone on hand at the moment to sing it anyway. "I'll wait until you do," replied Susan. "Send someone who can sing it to me as soon as you can."

The next day a young man delivered the message but Susan insisted he sing it to her. The young man protested saying she might better read the telegram herself but Susan was adamant.

"Sing it!" she insisted.

"OK, here it is." In a strong voice he began, "Your Uncle Fred is dead. The funeral is on Tuesday. Please omit the flowers. There will be no calling hours."

Overstepped That Time

I always liked to attend meetings and other affairs if there was a good chance of having refreshments afterwards. If one particular goodie was way above average I could usually get seconds or thirds by stating, "If I could find out who made this delicacy, I would try to talk her into running away with me." Most of the time that would gain me points with the ladies and usually the special cook would be someone I knew very well and not anyone who would run off with a man simply because he liked her baking skills. But it did produce a nice smile and most girls like to be appreciated. A few times my remarks resulted in my carrying home a whole box of whatever it was that took my fancy.

My wife and I went to church in a North Carolina town one Sunday and the service was followed by a sumptuous offering of cakes, pies, cookies and other delectable items. Those ladies tried to outdo each other and received many compliments. Of course, my usual offer to run away with whoever had the best of the lot raised some eyebrows but almost immediately the heroine appeared.

"This is my day," she declared, "I've waited years for a mature man. If there is any quality I like in a man it's maturity. Let's go right now before you change your mind." My mild but polite protests were to no avail. She was adamant. "You don't even have to go home to get anything. I'll buy you a whole new wardrobe and whatever else you need. Let's go. I like that white hair. I'm sick of immature men, come on!"

Thinking fast is not one of my best traits, but in front of those women, all curious as to how this would play out, I began to rack my brain for a way to extricate myself. Finally that 1,000-watt light bulb came on. "I have to go back to our town house. You see I never go away overnight without my teddy bear."

The woman whirled away from the table and growled, "Never mind, never mind, so much for maturity!"

New Techniques

When Ken Jones arrived home from his four years in the Army after traveling about the world and attaining the grade of tech sergeant, his father decided to take him down a peg. He didn't want any high and mighty ideas Ken might have picked up to disrupt the family discipline and he certainly didn't want anyone on the farm to take his place in the sun. Better to teach him a lesson in humility right away.

The next morning bright and early, the bossy old man roused the family and explained his plan to rehabilitate Ken. "Now son, we all want to get you back to where you were when you left us to go traipsing off around the world, filling your head with God knows what. So take this shovel and clean out the outhouse. I want it [the contents] spread evenly on that field over yonder so git to it."

Ken stared at the shovel and looked over at the large three-hole outhouse before addressing his father and the assorted family members that included several uncles gathered to see the re-indoctrination. "Now Paw, you must know I didn't spend four years in the Army without learning something about modern ways of doing things. For instance, I specialized in demolition and my knowledge of explosives shouldn't be wasted. Why don't you give me a chance to demonstrate some of my skills right here and now?"

The old man was somewhat boxed in as everyone else seemed interested to see what Ken had learned. He reluctantly agreed but made it clear there would be only one demonstration and if it failed everything would again be done according to Paw's rules.

Ken got his gear, strung out a hundred feet of fuse and attached it to a good supply of dynamite placed around the base of the solidly built structure. When everyone was safely hiding behind the big trees in the yard Ken pushed the plunger and triggered a gigantic explosion. The outhouse sailed up into the air like a rocket. The effluence was spread evenly over the designated field. As the building came whistling back down, Ken ignited his secondary charges and the outhouse settled smoothly and gently onto its foundation. The family was amazed and everyone crowded around Ken, congratulating him.

As the backslapping tapered off they heard a bumping and thumping until the outhouse door burst open. Grandpa staggered out pulling up his suspenders and shouting, "By grannies, it's a good thing I didn't let that one go in the kitchen!"

Florida Cracker

I once took a long bus ride from Florida to San Marcos, Texas. As we traveled the length of the Florida panhandle, a tall very thin character in threadbare overalls got on board and immediately started to regale the passengers about how he had survived a terrible accident when a train struck his truck and demolished it.

"That train hit my truck broadside and threw me out into a swamp, but the truck was rolled and dragged for a quarter-mile. Now I tell you, it was some wreck. Why, the cab was nothing but a piece of scrap metal, the transmission hit a telegraph pole so hard it broke it off, while the platform my two boys would have been riding on went sailing off into some trees beside the track.

"Both boys wanted to drive over to Pensacola to get some hog feeders and they argued so much I finally let them ride in the cab of the truck with me. With those big rascals in the cab I was squeezed right up against the door. It was a real good 1935 Dodge ton and a half and the best truck I ever had. Of course it was the only truck I ever had! It would go through mud up to the running board and deep sand didn't faze it a bit, good on gas, too, for the first ten years. Burned a little oil but always started up on the first crank."

All the passengers and the bus driver were mesmerized by the details of the wreck and were leaning forward in their seats to hear every word. At this point in his story the old boy stopped to get a chew of tobacco out of the pocket of his bib overalls. This gave the passengers their first chance to break in and ask the question everyone wondered about. What became of the boys? "Have your sons recovered from their injuries?" asked one elderly lady.

"Hell no! There weren't enough left of 'em to sort out and the only part of my truck we could find in one piece was the seat I was a settin' on. Them railroad men picked up all the trash from my truck before I could salvage it to sell for scrap iron. I tell you that was some wreck. I know I'll never find another truck as good as that old Dodge, no sir!"

One Was Missing

High up in the Appalachian Mountains, old Zeb had a hog farm and every so often he would take a load of hogs down to a market in eastern Tennessee. Zeb's five sons had very little social life and limited formal schooling so they always wanted to go with Zeb to see some of the outside world. They had to take turns when a load was sent down the mountain. The boys finally talked their father into letting them all take the load down by themselves. The old man reluctantly agreed, although he knew it was very dangerous since three of them would have to ride in the back of the truck with the hogs. He watched them leave with a sense of foreboding but hoped for a safe trip.

Halfway down the winding mountain road the brakes failed. The truck with its cargo plunged down a steep cliff and was demolished when it struck the bottom. It was some time before help arrived to take the boys to a hospital and then to decide what to do with the load of dead hogs scattered along a creek bed. Zeb managed to persuade a rendering plant to clean up the site and take the hog carcasses off to be turned into fertilizer.

Zeb's youngest son, Abe, was recuperating some weeks later in the shade of the big trees in the backyard. "Paw, I've been ciphering. Now Amos didn't make it and he's buried over there next to Ma. Noah and Jacob are still down in the hospital and I'm here talking to you. What bothers me is I can't add up to five of us. Where's Jude Paw? Do you suppose you might have been a bit too hasty sendin' them hogs down to the rendering plant?"

Note: They found Jude. He had been taken to a hospital clear over in Nashville.

Tough Love

Billy Joe came tearing up the trail that led to his shack perched high up on a mountaintop. His ancient, rusty pickup truck with the cab and rear box filled with cans, bottles, animal pelts and unidentifiable items, bounced over the rocks and old ruts. A Confederate flag and two rifles slung across the back window completed the picture. He skidded to a stop in front of the rickety porch and was surprised to see his wife standing there with her belongings stuffed into two plastic bags.

"What's goin' on here, Becky?" he asked.

"I'm leavin' you, Billy Joe. You never took me nowhere, you don't help me do nothin' round the house, you never talk to me and I've been stuck in this shack ever since we was married. I'm leavin' you, Billy Joe. You are always over in the holler with your drinkin' buddies or up to your still until all hours. And another thing, Billy Joe, you ain't nothin' but a no good *pedophile*!"

Her husband was speechless for a moment before responding. "*Pedophile*! That's a pretty big word coming from a twelve-year-old!"

Scores to Settle

The Jeters and the Colbys had been feuding for nearly two centuries over a boundary dispute. Gunfire erupted if one or the other set foot on the other's property, and whenever two or more members of the clans met on common ground, hard looks but no words passed between them. The two extensive properties were separated by a brook and because the two families had increased in numbers over the years, "overcrowding" was keeping everyone edgy. Space, they felt, was becoming critical. Their most tragic and violent encounter had occurred in the mid-1880s, which resulted in three deaths on each side, and exacerbated the animosity between the mountain people.

Caleb Colby was a handsome young man, skilled in the mountain work of cutting timber, hunting deer and making moonshine. His favorite pastime was fishing for trout in the brook marking the border of the properties. It was here the young man's thoughts would turn to his disappointment of not finding a mate. He wanted very badly to get married but eligible brides were nonexistent in the locality and his family had run out of cousins. He was deep in these thoughts as he fished one day in the brook running between the Jeters and the Colbys.

He was startled to see a girl bathing in a pool downstream from his location. As he began to appreciate the more pleasant aspects of the scene before him, he suddenly realized she was on the Jeter side of the brook. He approached her furtively and quietly until a dead branch snapped under his foot. The girl looked up terrified because very few people visited this part of the woodland but his kind face, strapping figure and gentle demeanor caught her attention. She had never seen such a good-looking man so she observed him as she put on her clothes behind a bush. She realized he must be a Colby as he remained on the opposite side of the stream but she was fascinated and quite excited so she cautiously entered into a dialogue with the handsome stranger.

Neither of them had been to school for more than a few days but of course they were able to communicate in the vernacular of mountain folk. Caleb finally made the observation she was the most beautiful person he had ever seen and she acknowledged by emphatically declaring he was the handsome man in her dreams. Finally they met in midstream and embraced, awkwardly at first, but soon were caught up in a passionate embrace.

It was nearly dusk when Caleb picked the girl up and "carried her off" towards his home. Her appearance the next morning caused some consternation among the Colby clan. However, after a few days the couple announced they wanted to get married and this brought fears of retaliation from the Jeters. This intermingling had never been tolerated before but a few older folks thought perhaps the union had a good chance of reconciling with their longtime adversaries and it was decided to take a chance. The local preacher would have no part of the marriage as he also feared retaliation from the Jeters. However, over the ridges to the east it was thought the new young minister there might be more agreeable, and so he proved to be.

It was a hike of many miles to get over the ridges but several of Caleb's relatives made the trek. They hoped their support of the young couple's marriage would improve relations between the long feuding clans. However, within a month after the wedding a band of Jeters attacked the cabin owned by Caleb's father, a strong mountain man, but unlettered and known to be obstinate at times. A few of the well-armed Colby kinsmen managed to take up positions in and around the cabin and returned the fusillade of lead from the Jeters. Most unfortunately, Caleb was seriously wounded within the first hour of the attack. "I'm hit Pappy, I'm hit bad!" moaned the son. His father continued firing all the while chewing on his tobacco.

"Pappy! I'm a goin'. I'm a goin' fast Pappy!"

Pappy, a seasoned veteran of the feud, continued shooting, pausing only to expectorate into a tin can in the middle of the cabin floor. "Take your time son, take your time."

A Ford is a Ford

A neighbor of mine was a Ford Motor Company disciple. He had driven and promoted Ford products for fifty years and would argue the merits of his chosen wheels at the drop of a hat. One day he accosted me and showed me his new Mercury and allowed there couldn't be a better car anywhere than a Ford product. I kept quiet about the new Mercury I had just acquired that was parked out of sight in the garage. I interrupted him in his praise of Ford cars to tell him a story about a farmer who put a new tin roof on his barn. Within weeks the tail end of a hurricane got under the edge of the new roof and soon lifted it completely off the barn. It sailed away and ended up a crumpled mass wedged into the rocks on the side of Snake Mountain.

Since it was wartime the farmer thought it would be patriotic to salvage the metal and send it for recycling. Getting together a group of boys from the nearby high school he managed to retrieve a box car load of tin and sent it off to Dearborn, Michigan.

Some weeks later he received a letter from Ford Motor Company: "Mr. Dunton, we don't know what happened to your car but if you will send us the model and serial number we will do our best to straighten it out."

My friend's jaw dropped, he stared at me a moment then stomped off to his house muttering, "It takes all kinds!"

Be Diplomatic, Be Tactful

The sergeant read off the duties for the day to his formation of soldiers. "Smith, you have a dental appointment, Jones, report for guard duty. The rest of you go to your training except you, Johnson, report to the orderly room to get furlough papers, your father died this morning. Dismissed!"

The captain saw how devastated poor Johnson was so he called in the sergeant and gave him a talking to. "Next time something like this happens, Sergeant, I'm telling you to be more compassionate, think of the man's feelings for God's sake! Be more tactful."

"Yes, Sir! I'll do that, Sir."

About a month later there was another tragedy. After reading the day's orders the sergeant hesitated for a moment then said, "All you men whose mother is still living take one pace forward. Not so fast, Smedly!"

One Solution to the Problem

After being brought up to be conservative of time, resources and energy it distressed me to see the waste and poor judgment so prevalent in the military when I first enlisted. As cadet candidates, a group of us was temporarily posted to an airfield in Tennessee for shots, orientation and to be issued uniforms. Our train had barely stopped rolling when a very loud and boorish sergeant started yelling, "Another load of damn Yankees, a whole trainload of Yankees!" He then ordered us over to a large box filled with coal and told us to pick it up and move it about twenty feet. It was very heavy, as much as twenty of us could lift with difficulty. While we gasped and strained to hold the box he told us to dump the coal out onto the ground and put the box back. "Now throw the coal back into the box," he directed in his southern drawl. We stared in disbelief until the sergeant threatened us with lifetime KP or some other punishment for disobeying an order. So, in our civilian clothes and no gloves or shovels we did his bidding, ending up as black as the coal itself. This introduction to the military made me wonder how we could ever win the war.

The next time we encountered the sergeant he was disciplining three new inductees because one of them had thrown a cigarette butt on the ground. After procuring shovels he ordered all three to dig a hole six feet deep to bury the cigarette butt. "Leave it uncovered for others to see and be warned," he told them.

About this time an officer approached and inquired what was taking place. "OK, but you had better get rid of that pile of dirt," ordered the officer as he walked away.

The sergeant scratched his head and finally told the young men, "All right, go dig a hole over there to put this dirt in."

Times Haven't Changed

Two Roman soldiers stationed far from home in Persia were discussing military service. As they stood on a bridge over a small stream idly tossing pebbles into the water, one of the veterans of many campaigns spoke of the disadvantages of the military life. "I'm getting a little tired of the constant strict routine and being away from home so much." His companion was a bit more enthusiastic and made the remark, "Well, the army wouldn't be so bad if it weren't for all the papyrus work."

A Most Obedient Student

Bernard was a good kid but inclined to be mischievous. On his first day of school his mother told the teacher if Bernard misbehaved, to slap the kid next to him. That will frighten him enough to stop causing trouble, she claimed. Bernard was still a challenge to each teacher as he progressed to the fourth grade. However, Miss Barnes took no nonsense from anyone and demonstrated that mindset by administering six lickings to Bernard in one day. He still acted up, doing no harm but disrupting the class with his humorous antics. In the afternoon Miss Barnes marched her unruly student to a corner of the room and told him not to leave that spot until she herself gave him permission. "No matter what happens, do not move from this spot until I personally give you permission." There was a screen closing off the corner to prevent the one being disciplined from distracting the class.

Somehow, Miss Barnes neglected to excuse Bernard when school let out so he remained quietly behind the screen until everyone had left. On his way home he thought of another trick to play on his teacher. When Miss Barnes arrived at her desk the next morning she was shocked to hear a plaintive voice coming from behind the screen. "Miss Barnes, may I go to the bathroom? I have to go right now!" It was the only time Bernard ever arrived at school before anyone else.

Go!

One of my first attempts at courting a girl took place on her parents' front porch. Almost everyone in those days had a glider on the porch that easily swung back and forth with little effort. It could seat three people but two fit nicely and as long as the glider kept swinging it made a familiar screeching sound. If the screeching stopped you could depend on the girl's mother to open the screen door to see what caused the silence. No hanky panky on gliders. I was too shy around girls to start anything and made sure the screeching didn't stop. However, on one evening, the girl stopped the swing and took my hand in hers. With a sweet smile she leaned close and whispered, "What would you do if you had money?" Thinking it over while keeping one eye on the screen door, I whispered back, "I guess I would travel." She slowly withdrew her hand and slipped into the house. I looked in my palm and there was a nickel!

The Big Letdown

Thelma was every boy's dream. She had a great figure, blonde hair, big blue eyes and was extremely well-endowed. There was a great deal of rivalry because she was so popular but it narrowed down to two young men who showered Thelma with attention, gave her gifts and entertained her lavishly. Finally Raymond won out over Ted and soon the couple was married. All the young men were envious and anxious to hear how Raymond was getting along with his new bride. Ted got up courage to ask Raymond what it was like to be married to Thelma. A downcast Raymond responded, "It's the greatest letdown of my life. I can't touch her. She's so ticklish she goes into hysterics if I put a hand on her."

It Really Worked!

Belle and Alan became involved in a multilevel sales scheme that specialized in health products. Belle was approaching forty years of age, so when the company began touting an elixir they claimed would stop the aging process she went for it in a big way although Alan had no interest at all. "Snake oil!" he called it. Belle, however, believed in it and imagined she looked and felt younger after several weeks of taking the overrated concoction. Observing herself in the mirror a few days before her birthday, she decided to go all the way and not just retard the aging process but regain her youthful appearance as well. She drank three bottles right after breakfast. When Alan came into the house Belle was crying her eyes out. "What's the matter, dear, what happened?" Between sobs and twisting her handkerchief, Belle finally wailed, "I missed my school bus!"

But It Really Did Work!

The owner of the factory (distillery-brewery) where the elixir of youth was manufactured felt so pleased with sales he decided to host an Open House. As he was regaling the crowd about the success users of his product had been reporting, an attendant refilled his glass. The poor man lost his balance and still holding his glass tumbled into one of the huge vats filled with a concentrated form of the secret to youthfulness. After a hectic rescue effort by the employees he was finally hauled out but the potion had done its work dramatically. Believers in evolution were delighted because the rescuers had pulled out a chimpanzee dressed in a tuxedo and still holding a cocktail glass!

Lucky Girl

Two old codgers, Bill and Amos, ran a small business over in New Hampshire. They would try to be out on the porch every afternoon about two o'clock to admire the town beauty as she walked down the street on her way home from work. She usually dressed in a provocative style and attracted quite a bit of attention as she promenaded down the length of the street. Men of all ages admired her and she was courted by many. The two old partners often commented on her appearance and how some lucky young man would eventually win her hand and heart.

Bill was gone for a week on business over in Albany and while he was away, Amos became a justice of the peace. His first duty in this capacity would be to marry Ella, the much sought after beautiful girl every one admired and desired. She planned to marry the young druggist in town. When Bill returned he and Amos sat on the porch to watch Ella walk gracefully down the street, Amos broke the news. "I'm going to marry that girl next week and I'm pretty excited about it."

Bill came out of his chair and began a tirade against his business partner. "You old fool, are you crazy? What are you thinking of—and what in the world is she thinking of?"

Bill didn't even stop for breath nor did he give Amos a chance to explain. He dashed off red-faced, ran as fast as he could and caught up with Ella just as she reached her home. "Ella, is it true Amos is going to marry you next week?" Bill panted.

"Yes he is," the girl said happily.

"If I give you three hundred dollars will you promise not to marry Amos?"

Thinking fast Ella thought to humor him by saying, "Sure, I promise not to marry Amos." So Ella was presented her first wedding present, three hundred dollars, by agreeing not to marry the new justice of the peace.

One Man's Solution

Up in Hardville, Vermont, two brothers had a thriving combination grocery and hardware store. One hot, sultry afternoon they took turns going down the street to an ice cream stand—orange pineapple for Ralph and maple walnut for Fred. Later, on making change for a customer, one of the brothers noticed ten dollars was missing from the cash register. Each one was convinced the other had taken the money while the other was getting his ice cream. This led to the first real argument the two had ever engaged in. The bitter war of words went on and fortunately ended without physical violence but they stopped speaking to each other. One purchased a second cash register while the other partner built a railing down the center of the store separating the hardware from the groceries. Neither former partner would wait on a customer in the other's department and not another word passed between them for eighteen years.

The local people accepted the arrangement because this wall of silence between two individuals was not uncommon and all too often between some husbands and wives. One woman on her death bed after twenty years of the silent treatment told family members present to tell her husband she loved him.

A traveling man was surprised to be told he couldn't purchase an item of hardware from the man behind the grocery counter. The hardware man was "out" he was informed. A bit curious, the stranger inquired around town about the strange business and was astounded to learn the two brothers had not spoken to each other all those years and yet maintained the two businesses separately.

Being a somewhat crafty opportunist, the traveling man began taking wagers from many of the townspeople saying he could get the two to make up and start talking again. Almost everyone was willing to risk a few dollars in the remote chance the two brothers could be reconciled. After accumulating a hefty bankroll and putting up security to repay the bets in case he was unsuccessful, the man re-entered the store and called the two over to the railing dividing the businesses. "Gentlemen," he began. "Almost twenty years ago, I was in this town, broke and hungry. I succumbed to temptation and took ten dollars from your cash drawer, an act that has bothered my conscience ever since. Here are the ten dollars and another ten for interest, goodbye and God bless you." The brothers stared at each other for a few moments, then embraced and wiped away a tear or two. The townspeople gladly paid off their bets and thanked the mediator profusely for reuniting the two popular citizens.

I Can Prove It

At the local historical society meeting the topic for the evening was the Indian wars of the West. The guest speaker concluded his presentation with an emotional account of Custer's last stand. When he stated as a historical fact that no one survived the battle, one man raised his hand and after being recognized, stated that his great-grandfather did, in fact, live through the famous engagement. The speaker adamantly disagreed with that statement remarking the man should re-read history. "My great-grandfather did survive the Battle of the Little Bighorn and my family still has the scalps to prove it!"

Longevity?

"How did you spend your weekend, Charles?"

"Oh we had a great family get-together celebrating my great-grandfather's one hundred twenty-first birthday."

"One hundred twenty-one years? Why that must be a record, but tell me, at that age was he able to attend the affair?"

"Oh no, he died when he was forty-four but we still get together to celebrate every year."

Take Your Pick

A small city up on the Canadian border had only two restaurants and they were not very appealing. One afternoon I was strolling along the shore of beautiful Lake Memphremagog when a man approached me and asked which of the two eating places should he choose for a good meal. Meditating on my experiences with each one, I answered, "Well let me put it this way: Whichever one you select, you will wish you had chosen the other one."

Welcome to Massachusetts

A family of in-laws used to brag about their ancestors arriving on the Mayflower at Plymouth Rock. After tiring of hearing the same old story one member of our family made a response. "Well, that's something to be proud of but my ancestors met the boat when your people landed and fed them all winter. They were dedicated 'hippies' and didn't know anything about surviving in the wilderness. Of course, modern day hippies usually have well-to-do parents to furnish them with money but the Pilgrim hippies had only us to depend on for their needs that first winter. Their communal lifestyle just didn't work out for them either. Heck, your folks hadn't even heard of corn but we taught them how to plant it and use it. Aren't you glad we were there to meet them?"

Authentic?

A "collector of coins" was trying to raise enough money for a six-pack of beer by offering a genuine 2100-year-old Roman coin.

"How can you prove it is that old?" one prospective buyer asked.

"Why look at it, it's stamped right here, 117 B.C."

More Fodder for Ridicule

My grandchildren in their teens and early twenties took great delight in making fun of me. To them I was just a doddering, forgetful old "duffer" who couldn't remember where his car was parked and looked everywhere for his glasses before discovering he was still wearing them. Because they generated so much laughter, I played along with them to a degree. "Grandpa, this is the nineties," or another time they exclaimed, "Grandpa, come on out with us to see Halley's Comet. Oh, sorry, you've already seen it twice, haven't you?" During dinner, one of them asked, "Do you want me to cut your meat for you, Grandpa?" At my seventy-fifth birthday party, they were reveling in their favorite pastime and having a great time at my expense until I decided to really give them something to get mileage out of. "Hold it!" I said. "Stop right now and listen to me. When I was your age we all had to..., we had to..., let's see now...there was *something* we had to do...."

Humor in the Cockpit

Occasionally, even the pilot pushes the wrong button such as when the captain of an airliner called the stewardess. "Honeybunch, bring me a mug of coffee and some of your passionate ever-loving self," he instructed. He didn't realize his message was being broadcast over the intercom to all the passengers. Honeybunch, working in the rear of the plane, was not only embarrassed but, dreading any further intimate messages from the captain, started on a dead run for the cockpit. As she slowed her mad dash to open the door a lady in the front seat put her hand on her arm and said, "Honey, you forgot the coffee."

Get Ready!

On a flight back from Washington, D.C., I was flying the plane while five other National Guard officers were visiting and relaxing. One of them noticed the commander of our group was sleeping soundly in his seat. Right away the others decided to play a trick on the sleeping colonel so they all put parachutes on and stood up in the aisle as if they were about to abandon ship. When one of them woke the sleeping officer he quickly took in the scene and made a desperate effort to get his chute on and started a dash for the door. Fortunately the others blocked his way and calmed him down, much to his chagrin. It would have been hard to explain if he had managed to bail out over the southern tip of Lake Champlain, but "Fly Boys" have a history of playing tricks.

Temptation

On a long flight across Canada, Fred couldn't take his eyes off of a stewardess with a devastatingly voluptuous figure. Fred had an aisle seat and as she leaned across him to adjust the tray at the window seat he couldn't resist a little pat. "Watch that, Mister!" she said ominously. "I have, for an hour and forty-five minutes," answered Fred.

Pilot Error?

Following a few fatal airline crashes, government officials, the FAA, bureaucrats and congressmen organized an investigation to be held in California. They were all mostly from Washington, D.C., but saw an opportunity to travel and indulge in a little high living at government expense. During their brief meetings to consider possible solutions, the term "pilot error" came up all too frequently. The day before leaving, they reluctantly ended the night life and an official report was hastily prepared and shared with the media. The consensus was that pilot error contributed the most to the accidents and a crash program should be initiated to develop more automated control of passenger airliners. Pilots across the country were incensed and highly insulted but decided to take some kind of action to expose the ignorance of the bureaucrats.

After the Washington geniuses finally boarded the plane and had consumed their first few drinks, the voice of the captain came on welcoming them aboard for the long flight across the continent. "We want you gentlemen to feel especially safe on this flight because this aircraft is completely automated and every phase of its operation is controlled by one of the new computers. This relieves the pilot and co-pilot of all duties as you cruise along at 500 miles an hour at 37,000 feet. The automation is so complete there is no need for the crew to be with you. In fact, we are on the ground here in Los Angeles and this message is reaching you by the cockpit tape. You gentlemen are very aware that electronics are much more reliable than human pilots and will bring an end to 'pilot error' accidents. You should feel very safe and secure because with the technology you recommended, nothing could go wrong...could go wrong...could go wrong...could go wrong...."

Don't Look

During helicopter training students are required to practice forced landings over and over. The maneuver is called "auto rotation." The procedure was to close the throttle to simulate engine failure then lower the pitch of the rotor (the angle the rotor blade bites the air) to cause the rotor to gain speed as the machine drops rapidly towards the ground. About six or eight feet from the ground the pitch is pulled up sharply, the rotor blades bite the air effectively and have the effect of slowing the rate of descent. Forward motion (air speed) of the chopper has to be maintained during the rapid descent so the pilot can slide along the ground and come to a stop safely.

It is a very hair-raising event the first few times the instructor takes a student through the lifesaving maneuver. With practice the pilot becomes proficient enough to save his life in the event of an actual engine failure. At night, this becomes even more interesting because the terrain may not be ideal for a safe landing. However, a light under the nose of the craft helps a pilot to choose, at the last seconds, the best area available. During a briefing session before a night flight the instructor asked the class, "What would you do if you are going down at night and your light reveals a power line directly ahead? How would you feel when you saw those high-tension wires? What would you do?" One student had what he thought was an answer. "I would turn the light off!"

A Shaky Start

A young student pilot who had taken a much longer time than others to master the airplane was finally told by the reluctant instructor to take his first solo. More nervous than ever, the student made a sloppy takeoff and proceeded to fly some hair-raising maneuvers above the airport, completely disoriented. Finally the tower operator called him and asked, "What's the name of that pilot up there?" With a shaky voice the student answered, "There isn't any pilot. I'm up here all alone!"

Good News/Bad News

The pilot on an international flight addressed the passengers over the loud speaker. "I have some bad news and some good news," he announced in a slight Mediterranean accent. "The bad news is we are lost, but the good news is, we are making excellent time!"

Blind Pilots

Passengers on an airliner were startled to see the pilot come aboard wearing sunglasses and using a white cane followed by the co-pilot holding onto a seeing-eye dog. They entered the cockpit, closed the door and started the engines. People thought it was just a trick but were apprehensive. As the plane roared down the runway, still not airborne, agitation built and passengers began to scream and as the end of the runway approached, the screams became shrill and panicky. "We are going to crash! We are going into the water!" Just then the plane lifted smoothly into the air and everyone relaxed—for a moment. The pilot spoke to his co-pilot making sure the cabin speakers were on. "You know, Fred, if they don't start screaming sooner we will end up in the water. I was getting a little nervous back there."

Comforting to Know

Passengers on a transatlantic flight were uneasy when the pilot announced they had lost one of the four engines. However, they were reassured when the pilot told them everything was alright but they would arrive at their destination one hour late. Shortly afterwards, a second engine failed. "Not to worry folks. We can continue our flight safely but now we will be two hours late." When a third engine quit the passengers began to be very concerned but again the pilot comforted them by saying the plane could safely carry on but now they were looking at a three-hour delay for arrival. One passenger poked his seatmate with his elbow and remarked, "If we lose another one, we will be up here all day!"

A Little Known Fact

During World War II there was much rivalry between crews on B-17 bombers and B-24s. Back in 1943 I was trying to save money on a change of stations so I looked for a flight in some kind of military aircraft rather than taking a long train ride. A B-24 Liberator bomber was ready to leave for an airbase a short distance from my destination. I thought, "This will be an opportunity to see the difference in the two aircraft." The plane looked awkward to me after being so comfortable with the appearance and handling of our beautiful B-17 Flying Fortress.

I was surprised when a crewman handed me a set of coveralls and told me to put them on over my Class-A uniform. It was astonishing to see everyone else dressed the same and holding shovels! Some of the men were quite dirty, covered with what looked like coal dust. The co-pilot handed me a clipboard, told me to read it carefully and sign the paper. It was an oath of secrecy stating that all on board this B-24 were never to reveal any details of the flight or the operation of the aircraft. Wow! It sounded like a real adventure so I signed. As we started to taxi out, a door to the rear bomb bay opened revealing a large pile of coal and we were told to start shoveling. This flying monstrosity burned coal!

By the time we reached MacDill Field in Tampa, Florida, we were all covered with coal dust and completely exhausted. The co-pilot reappeared in his spotless uniform and admonished me to take very seriously the document I had signed. After turning in the shovel, gloves and coveralls in a mental haze it occurred to me what all the secrecy was about. The outside world was not to be aware that some B-24s burned coal! That was sixty-five years ago and to this day you will never hear a B-24 crewman admit they had to shovel coal to keep the old "boxcars" flying.

Note: The B-24 was an excellent plane for some purposes. There was a ditty that went around the B-17 bomb groups in England that was quite derogatory concerning the B-24. It suggested the B-17s were more dependable for longer missions due to their ability to take damage but still complete the long missions and return safely. It went: "All the forts (B-17 flying fortresses) to Berlin the newspapers say, while the B-24s hit the Pas de Calais." Berlin was a 600-mile trip while the Pas de Calais, just across the English Channel, was almost within sight of the B-24's home base.

From the Farm

Teddy was the first in his family, in fact, the first in his neighborhood to win an international prize—or so they thought for a while. Teddy had a magnificent rooster, Ervin, that he had raised from an egg and won several awards when he showed it at 4-H, the Field Days and finally at the State Fair. As the county agents from the extension service judged the bird they were amazed at its beauty, size and majestic appearance. As they were about to award the blue ribbon an old farmer stepped up and asked permission to examine the bird. He gave it a thorough examination and announced, "This 'rooster' is the first one of his gender capable of laying eggs." So Teddy was awarded the "Pullet Surprise."

Something Overlooked

An army officer retired with the rank of colonel and many awards due mainly to his knowledge of military regulations. He had spent most of his career taking advantage of the many perks available to those who took time away from their duties to study the tricks to be promoted and win citations. He was accused of "writing the regulations."

Now he could begin his lifelong ambition to have a farm. He decided to raise "purebred polled longhorn steers." In no time at all a local cattle dealer sold him ten steers to start his herd, not mentioning to the would-be farmer-rancher that steers have no way to reproduce, nor did he let on that they were, in fact, polled shorthorn steers and, of course, polled cattle never develop horns, something the buyer was not aware of. The naive retired officer then proceeded to build a strong fence around a field that was to be his pasture. The grass was green and luxuriant but the poor steers just stood at the fence and bellowed day and night. With much effort they were corralled and an expensive visit by the local veterinarian turned up nothing but a comment that they looked gaunt, which was odd because of the plentiful grass they had access to. Finally, the former owner of the farm heard of the problem and paid a visit. Looking aghast at the poor animals he shouted, "You damned fool, there's no water in that field!"

Smart Pig

A career-long friend of the colonel bought a nearby small farm to raise hogs and, having studied the start-up procedures, he bought a sow and looked around for someone who had a boar hog to breed his sow. His background studies covered the breeding cycle of hogs and he was pleased to learn the gestation period was only a few weeks so he could expect eight or perhaps twelve little pigs quite frequently. This seemed like a profitable enterprise.

A neighbor, Maggie, who was somewhat of a weird character, had a boar and agreed to accommodate him if he could transport the sow to her farm. Visiting Maggie was an interesting experience as she had strange habits. One very annoying trait was lighting her cigarette by striking her match on an unsuspecting man's zipper. She had apparently misinterpreted the name of the popular brand of Zippo lighters.

After wheeling the heavy sow down the road in a two-wheeled cart and back again after the deed was accomplished, the would-be farmer felt exhausted. Checking the sow a few weeks later he was dismayed to not find any little pigs, so down the road with the sow in the cart to his new friend who gladly accepted his fee for the service. This went on for some time until someone with a little compassion informed him that the sow had to be "in the mood," which took a little explaining. "You will know she is in the mood when she starts acting strange, something out of the ordinary."

By the time she was in the mood the sow had gained considerable weight and her owner dreaded wheeling her down the road again and even anticipated a struggle to load her into the cart. He had been careful to watch for signs of any strange behavior.

One morning he was surprised to find her sitting in the cart when he entered the barn. He decided this was a sign she was "in the mood."

The Affectionate Cow

A dairy farmer took on a hired hand who was very good with cows. He paid attention to each one by giving a pat on the head and talking to them while feeding or milking the animals. The farmer was quite pleased as he saw how much quieter and docile the whole herd had become due to the kindness of the new hired man. One cow, Bessie, seemed to take a liking to her new caretaker and would turn her head around in the stanchion while he was milking, never taking her eyes off him. She would gently bunt him whenever he walked through the barnyard and was noticeably irritable and uneasy whenever the man took his weekend off and someone else did the chores.

Before long, people heard about the friendship that had developed between the cow and the man who showed her so much kindness and there was so much teasing it led to harsh words between the boss and his worker because the farmer had joined in on the harassing of the best cowman they had ever seen in the area.

When the man told his boss to back off or he would leave, he had picked a time when the farmer was in a feisty mood that led to his remarking, "Pack up and go, the quicker the better!"

The hired man was quite surprised but kept his wits about him long enough to respond, "I'll go but you have to sell me that cow. I'm taking her with me!"

A few weeks later, the man the farmer had bought the cow from stopped by and noticed Bessie was gone. While discussing the circumstances of the cow's departure they were both surprised to discover the extraordinary dairyman who was so good with cows had worked for the former owner as well. "He was the best man with cows I've ever known," said the visitor. "In fact, he was working for me when that cow was born and took care of her for several months after. No wonder the cow liked him. She remembered him from the time she was a calf!"

Security for Two

A farmer went over his accounts very carefully and realized he was out of money. There was nothing left to pay his hired man who was so essential to the farm operation. Reluctantly, he broke the news to his faithful worker, Levi. Levi scratched his head, rubbed his chin and slipped his thumbs through his suspenders in deep thought. "Tell you what, Boss, why don't I work for you without pay until you owe me as much as the farm is worth, then I'll take over the farm and you work for me until you have earned it back. You see, that way, one of us will always have a job and one of us will always own a farm. What do you think about that idea?"

"Sounds good to me," replied the farmer. "We can see a lawyer and get papers drawn up with all the details." So the two men enjoyed security for many years.

Something Like the Golden Egg

A farmer had a magnificent work horse but in a moment of weakness he sold the animal to his neighbor for a price he felt he couldn't turn down. Before long he regretted having made the transaction so much he called on the neighbor, Fred, and pleaded with him to sell the horse back. They negotiated for some time until finally an outrageously inflated price was agreed upon and the horse was led back to his old home. Before many months passed Fred realized he had let the best horse he had ever owned go. He was tormented so much he strolled into his neighbor's yard one morning and made an emotional plea to buy the horse back. Again the two tossed figures back and forth until Fred pulled out a huge sum of cash and was handed the halter rope from his tearful brother-farmer. This swapping back and forth went on for years and each time the horse changed ownership the amount of money involved reached staggering sums.

Finally, on his watch, Fred succumbed to a fantastic offer for the, by now, shared property and word got around to his trading partner that Fred had sold out to a total stranger. People round about anticipated harsh words were about to pass between the two men. Fred listened to his heartbroken neighbor and sympathized with him, even offering comforting observations about the whole affair. "My good friend," Fred began. "Consider this, our horse had excellent care between us for all these years and is now getting on in age. Just think of all the money you and I have made. The price practically doubled each time we traded. How else could we have made such a good living all these years?"

"You are right," his friend responded, "But to make all of our past transactions equitable we should share this last profit, don't you think?"

"But of course we should." And the two men shook hands.

Old-Time Bankers

During my thirty-five years of farming, visiting a banker to borrow money was usually an ordeal. There was always a constant demand for more working capital but those old-time bankers tried to make you feel as if it was their money you were trying to use. One of these characters was very egotistical and arrogant. He had just had an artificial eye installed and was quite proud of the fact that hardly anyone could tell which eye was the real one. He made an effort to keep both eyes turned toward the person he was addressing and avoided glancing about because the fake eye would, of course, not move in sequence with the real one.

On one of my quests to enhance my checking account he abruptly turned me down although my credit standing had always been fairly good. My arguments for him to reconsider were to no avail until he caught me staring at his eyes. Because of his pride he offered me a deal. "If you can tell me which eye is the artificial one I will grant your loan but you have only five seconds."

Immediately I responded, "It's the left one."

"How could you tell in such a short time?" he gasped in surprise.

"When I asked for the loan and explained why I needed it, I saw a little sympathy in that eye."

Another old banker was very hard of hearing and always turned off his hearing aid until I finished explaining why I needed the money.

As a beginning young farmer I had a mortgage with a bank and never missed a payment but a farm across the road came on the market and it seemed to me like a good acquisition. In spite of my good track record the directors turned me down so I walked across the park and talked to the president of the rival bank. After explaining my request I was surprised when the old gentleman asked me if I wanted to buy it "on paper"—in other words, no down payment. Although I did have enough in my savings for the usual down payment I considered how helpful it would be to have that money in reserve to improve the new property. When I responded in the affirmative, this banker pulled out a blank piece of paper from a drawer and wrote down the amount of the loan and the terms of the contract with a short stub of a pencil. No meeting with bank directors—just a plain one-on-one business transaction. Throughout the period of the loan this banker kept track of my payments on the back of that sheet of paper with his old pencils.

The reaction from my primary bank was shocking. They notified me to present myself to their offices to lecture me on straying from the grip they had on me by the scruff of the neck. "You hurt us very badly," the head cashier told me.

"Then why did you turn me down when I offered to borrow the money from you?"

He made a vague explanation of loyalty but it fell on deaf ears. However, it was brought to my attention by another client that great animosity had already existed between the two institutions to the extent that a nice lady from the bank across the park had the door slammed in her face when she came to deliver some documents. Thankfully, banks today tend to be very polite to everyone.

Can't Get There From Here?

About six miles above my farm in the little city of Vergennes, Vermont, the main north-south highway made a sharp left turn from the main street at the only stoplight. The main street continued straight on down a hill and many travelers found themselves on Route 22A that led southwest, a kind of "Y" off the main highway. Usually by the time they reached my place they would have a feeling things weren't quite right. Out-of-state drivers, should they stop to inquire the way, half expected to be told by Vermonters, "You can't get there from here."

As I worked beside the road one day a huge black car, long enough to be registered in two states pulled up. When the electric window slid down I pulled my straw hat down a little and put a stalk of hay in my mouth to look more the part of the country bumpkin. A well-dressed man leaned over and very condescendingly said, "My good man, I'd like to get over to Bennington."

I chewed on the hay a couple of times before responding, "I have no objection."

Ironwood?

While traveling through the upper peninsula of Michigan en route to an important business meeting in Ironwood, George Norman and his wife decided to take a scenic route as there was more than enough time to make the conference scheduled for 8 p.m. After about an hour of driving through mostly forested country the road changed from paved to gravel and they noticed there were very few homes or farms. By the time they realized they were lost it was late afternoon and the couple began to worry as there were no places to inquire for directions. Coming to a fork in the road they stopped to study a map when they saw a man cutting wood up on a steep hillside.

George decided to climb up to speak with the woodcutter. Up a steep roadside bank, through a barbed wire fence and patches of thorn bushes he huffed and puffed until he reached the top of the hill. "Good afternoon, I need directions to Ironwood. Can you help me?" he inquired of the man who responded with a strong accent.

"Geez! Ironwood? You know, I neber been down dere." Further questions provided no help at all so George made his way back down the treacherous slope tearing his trousers on the thorns and barbed wire.

His wife said, "Look at your shoes! You've got them all mud. You are a sight to show up at the meeting, and remember, you have to give your report."

"We have to find the place first!" her exasperated husband reminded her.

"Oh look," she said, "There's another man up there now and they are motioning for you to come back. They must have figured out how to get us out of here."

Reluctantly, but getting somewhat alarmed, George started back up through the barbed wire fence and the thorn bushes scratching his legs and tearing his clothes on the way. When he reached the two men, the first one he had spoken to, put his arm across his companion's shoulder and proudly announced, "Dis here is my brudder Arno and you know someting? He neber been down dere needer!"

Dangers of Research

In the late 1970s some Middle Eastern countries were harassing us by taking Americans as hostages. One Muslim country, known for its hatred towards and envy of the United States jailed three men who were in the country to help make life better for the people. One was a farmer who was trying to improve agriculture; another, a priest, was hoping to establish ecumenical ties; a volunteer research scientist made up the third victim. Their treatment while incarcerated was so severe the authorities decided they should be executed to prevent them from telling the world about the atrocities.

It was decided to use an antiquated guillotine and the priest was dragged out first and was about to be strapped down in the conventional manner. "No, no, not that way. I want to die looking up to heaven. Place me on my back." The heavy steel blade was raised to the top of the tower and released but the razor-sharp device stopped about four inches from the priest's throat. "He's a holy man, let him go free," shouted the crowd of onlookers. In no time the lucky priest was in a taxi on his way to the airport.

When the farmer observed this, he thought the priest might have someting going so he also requested to be placed on his back. His captors accommodated him and again the blade stopped just in time. "Another holy man," the crowd shouted. "Let him go free as well." The farmer wasted no time getting to the airport.

When the research scientist was brought out he was placed on his back because the executioners thought all Americans must be crazy. As the blade was raised to the top of the tower the scientist looked up at it and spoke up. "Wait a minute, hold it! I think I see your problem."

No Way!

Henry decided to become an electrician and started work as an apprentice for a man who had twenty-five years experience in the field. The first job was to repair the electric chair at the Vermont State Prison over in Windsor. After several hours work everything had been checked out except for testing the morbid contraption. "Hop up there and let's see if this thing works," ordered the instructor. Not getting a response he looked around and could see his apprentice had disappeared. There was a gaping hole in the wall where Henry had made his speedy escape.

Limericks and Such

A wonderful skater was Rose
She could skate on the tips of her toes
She tried to show Clancy
Some steps that were fancy
But fell on the end of her nose.

Old Mother Hubbard went to the cupboard
To get her poor daughter a dress
When she got there the cupboard was bare
And so was her daughter I guess.

The Ford was the first of my "automobils"
Though it suffered from numerous ills

It could coast through the valleys
And scoot though the alleys
But had to be towed up the hills.

The Ford is my auto
I shall not want another
The rods and shafts discomfort me
The radiator runneth over
It maketh me to lie down beneath it.
I have replaced nearly every part
Yea, though I stop beside still waters
To stroll through the green pastures
I am forced to walk home
When the engine refuses to start.

When I was young and in my teens
I wore a pair of old blue jeans
The pant legs were all torn
And the knees were well worn
But I wish I could revisit those scenes.

I'm not into writing those nursery rhymes
I'm inclined to be involved with more serious crimes
Like telling bad jokes
And taking funny pokes
At people and places and times.

Sicnarf Reigna (you know this guy)

A member of my family was banished from the state of
Vermont and from the town where he had lived for over forty
years. Although he had been an exemplary citizen it mattered
not to his judges. Because of this harsh treatment he moved to
another part of the state after his banishment and changed his
name to Sicnarf Reigna.

One has to know something of the character of real Vermonters to understand how they could banish a longtime resident who paid his taxes, voted and kept out of trouble. According to *Vermont Life*, these people seldom smile, never eat quiche or yogurt, seldom leave the state, don't dodge potholes and never wear illustrated T-shirts.

Sicnarf did not live up to all of these native traits and was once unjustly accused of casting the first two Democrat votes in town. The board of civil authority just didn't believe there could be *two* democrats in town and said he must have voted twice. For this grievous offense his name was removed from the checklist, thereby preventing him from voting in that town for a period of twenty years.

However, the crime for which he was banished was far more serious, an unpardonable offence for any frugal Vermonter who was supposed to live within his means. When my wife and I were in Florida one winter we were invited by the Vermont Society to enjoy a picnic lunch at the St. Petersburg Municipal Pier attended by quite a few native Vermonters. We noticed Sicnarf sitting by himself over at one side and wondered why he was shunned by fellow Vermonters even in Florida. When we inquired the reason for this treatment one informed us, "Well! He dipped into his principal!"

At the Edge of My Grave

One summer I was feeling poorly and thought it was time to purchase a burial plot. There were four spaces adjoining my parents, grandparents and assorted uncles and aunts in the cemetery in what I called my home parish in Bristol, Vermont, nearly a hundred miles from my home, at the time, up in Newport. My appointment with the supervisor of the burial ground came up on a very hot day and just when I was not feeling well at all. Unable to reach him to postpone the meeting, I decided to go anyway and our oldest son, John, agreed to drive me down.

The temperature was hovering in the high nineties by the time we had nearly completed our business. A large funeral procession approached and gathered around the plot next to mine so we joined the crowd of perhaps over a hundred people, many I had known from the years I'd lived in the area. After nearly everyone had left for cooler places and we had concluded our transaction, two grave diggers I had known for some years came over and asked me if I felt all right. "No, I don't," I answered. "Did you just buy this plot?" one of them queried. When I answered in the affirmative they wanted to know if I still lived way up there on the Canadian border. Although feeling weak, not tolerating the heat very well and really not interested in prolonging the discussion, I admitted to still living there. After looking at the gravesite and scrutinizing me closely one of them observed, "It will hardly pay you to go way back up there, will it?"

Fooled Them That Time

When my wife and I decided to move to our town house in North Carolina after forty- seven years on the farm, we rented the house and packed up. In the evening we left in two vehicles. My wife drove the car loaded with some of our most valuable possessions while I followed with the big fully loaded moving van. After we were out of sight the townspeople gathered at the Grange Hall to celebrate. They were singing over and over, "Thank God and U Haul they are gone," but we had the last laugh because we used Ryder.

Don't Always Follow Instructions

On a business trip to Maine I deviated from the most direct route to see some of the back country and although not really lost it seemed prudent to ask someone for the most direct route back to better roads. An older farmer was just about to start plowing a little field surrounded by stone walls so after greeting him and admiring his beautiful team of horses, I inquired how best to get over to Farmington. "You want to git over to Faminton do you, well I'll tell you. Just go up here to the height of the land and you will come to the Congregational church where they have the annual chicken pie supper. Take a right turn there and go past the cemetery to a fork in the rud. Try the left one and you will go by the widow Thompson. She makes the best apple pies in Hancock County. She lives on the Bailey turnpike and down that rud there is a covered bridge that burned down in '37 or maybe '38, turn off towards Bull Moose Mountin about three mile this side of where the bridge used to be. Go through the beech woods and you will come out on a main rud. Just follow the signs from there to Faminton, or you can take the short cut from the first big red barn you come to on your left."

Trying very hard to remember his explicit directions I ignored the information about chicken pie suppers, apple pies and the nonexistent bridge to better concentrate on which "rud" to choose. Some three hours later I passed through what seemed like a familiar country road and sure enough, there was the farmer just about to finish plowing his little field. It was one of the few times when my temper flared out of control. Gathering up rocks to bounce off from his head, I started towards him yelling, "You old fool, you sent me around a three-hour circle for nothing!"

"Now just calm down, Capt'n, I'll tell you how to git to Faminton. You see I had to find out fust if you could follow instructions."

Sybil Bryant

In the late 1960s and early '70s I worked a territory from Erie, Pennsylvania, to the northern tip of Maine—over a thousand miles to travel often over country roads. My efforts as Marketing Area Chief for the National Farmers Organization were to help farmers work together for better prices for their produce. The odometer on my big powerful Chrysler sedan showed over 250,000 miles after only a little more than four years of intensive travel. For this reason, I was always looking for the shortest routes from one place to the next as well as using the telephone to plan my next day's work. There were no cell phones then so it was frequently necessary to use pay phones with the usual annoying delays and expense.

One morning while crossing the central part of New Hampshire on my way to Maine I realized a very influential farmer and business man lived somewhere in that vicinity—a person who might be willing to help his brother farmers if I were to speak to him about our struggle for fair prices. To save wandering around I decided to call him but there were no pay phones in the sparsely settled area so, noticing a very large Colonial house, I decided it wouldn't be unreasonable to ask to use their phone. The home was on a high rise of ground with fantastic views of lakes and valleys in all directions. A moderately sized orchard covered the slopes around the house. The names, "Virgil and Sybil Bryant," were on the mailbox.

A very healthy, robust woman perhaps in her mid-fifties answered the door and while she listened to my request regarding use of her telephone, an aroma of fresh baked and baking apple pies took my breath away. "I don't usually admit strangers but you look like an honest man so come in and you will find the phone at the far end of the parlor near the bay window." Walking through the spacious kitchen that held two very large stoves and some good-sized tables covered with fresh baked pies made me almost dizzy because of the wonderful aroma. The person who answered the phone said the man would call back in twenty minutes.

I took the chance that Sybil Bryant would allow me to wait for the call. She was very gracious and gave me quite a bit of history. She had been an officer in the Marine Corps during World War II and had married Virgil Bryant after returning home. Virgil was a perfectionist and ran his orchard in a way that produced bountiful crops of high quality apples.

Sybil started baking and selling apple pies, applesauce and a wonderful vinegar her husband put up in several barrels. Vans came from nearby Lake Winnipesaukee, from Keene and other cities and resorts to pick up hundreds of her famous pies. "Open that door to the cellar but watch your step and you will see our storage area," she told me. Another delightful odor emanated from the lower level. A hundred wooden barrels, filled with apples, sat on raised racks above the dirt floor. A dozen cider barrels were lined up along one wall giving off the musty fragrant smell of vinegar.

The apples kept all winter so Sybil had the fruit to make apple pies until summer when strawberries, raspberries and blueberries became available. "I never use frozen or canned fruit for my pies and I put a pad of *butta* on top before covering with the top crust. I also add just a jigger of vinegar for each pie but don't you tell anyone about that, hear?" I accepted the admonition to keep her secret but wondered why she told *me*. After my phone call was returned she explained she always used apple tree wood and oak to heat her ovens. Never before had I ever had such a lesson in baking or the care and use of apples by a "cook extraordinaire."

It was a delightful encounter but it was time for me to get on with my business. The crispy clean lady in her starched apron and sparkling well-lighted kitchen was something to remember. As I started for the door she pulled out a small pie and placed it in a box. "This is my husband's favorite. It's made with apples and apricots and I thought you might like it for your lunch after it cools down." With profuse thanks I accepted her gift!

My travels never took me up that road again and I probably couldn't find it if I tried unless the wind happened to blow that wonderful aroma across the hills and valleys of central New Hampshire.

High-Priced Lambs

On one of my active duty tours we were stationed in Texas in a charming little town and we were lucky enough to rent a house on a dead-end street that was surrounded by lush green alfalfa fields. For want of something different to do, the wives got together at the officer's club and decided to try their hand at dyeing clothes. This resulted in some colorful outfits for the ladies and for some of the children as well. Madeleine had the ideal place to practice her new hobby as the green fields around the house kept the dust from blowing onto her creations.

One day, she had a whole clothesline filled with material to dye and a large tub of baby blue dye sitting nearby. A playful lamb came romping down the lane and plopped into the tub. It was a beautiful sight to see the little animal playing around after he had dried off, his new blue coat flashing in the sun. Before the owner came looking for the lamb, someone driving down a nearby road saw the novelty and pulled into our street. They offered my wife a hundred dollars for the lamb and she sold it as soon as the owner came by and told her he wouldn't think of having that blue lamb back in his flock.

Madeleine started buying lambs and soon offered every color imaginable for sale to willing buyers. It became a full-time enterprise and before long Madeleine became the biggest lamb dyer in Texas.

Big is Big

A Texan touring Vermont struck up an acquaintance with a farmer who had a very modest-sized farm. The visitor ridiculed every aspect of the Vermonter's property. "Two hundred acres. Why, my vegetable garden is bigger than that. Fifty cows! I stopped counting my herd of cattle when I reached fourteen thousand." He was taken aback to learn that the family still used an old outhouse in the backyard. "We have four bathrooms at our ranch house and all I have to do is pull on a fancy chain and tons of water flush everything out of sight. Tell you what, old timer, you all come on down to my place in Central Texas at my expense and see how we live."

The farm family took the train from Essex Junction, Vermont, out to Texas and were astonished at the size of everything. The tall Texan wasn't lying to them, just bragging as they could see for themselves. Just after dark the old farmer really needed to find the bathroom and just assumed they were located in the backyard as he was accustomed to at home. He went out the back door and fell into the swimming pool. As he struggled to stay on top of the water he panicked and yelled out as loud as he could, "Don't flush it! Don't flush it!"

Been There

Paul was a talker for his age and was noted for his ability to describe things in detail. The townsfolk decided to send Paul down to New York City right after his graduation from high school so they would know what it was like. They saw him off on the train, anticipating a good report when Paul returned as no one from the community had ever been to a big city. A week later Paul returned and everyone gathered at the Grange hall to hear what New York City was really like. Paul took the stage and related all the details of the train ride down and back as well as Grand Central Station. Then someone asked him to get down to business and tell about the city. "Well," Paul said "There was so much going on at the depot I never did get to see the village."

Whoops

Miss Abigail Kingsley worked on the family farm and cared for her parents until she was in her late fifties. After both her father and mother passed away she inherited the farm so she sold the cattle and machinery to have a well-earned rest but soon became bored. She also began to dwell on her lifelong lack of a social life and after reading about lifestyles in the big cities she began to feel adventurous and ready to make up for lost time. She gave her cat and canary away, sold the one hundred and fifty acre farm and relocated to Dallas, Texas.

Abigail soon began a whirlwind round of parties and events where she became quite well known and was quite popular after some minor cosmetic improvements and radically changed dressing styles.

A little flirting with men her age and older finally brought her in contact with a very wealthy man. She was curious about how he had acquired his money. "Were you in the oil business, Sir?"

"No, M'am," came the reply.

"Oh then, perhaps you were a rancher."

Again the man answered, "No, M'am."

Abigail was really curious now so she came right to the point. "Well, in what business *did* you make your money?"

"Land, M'am, land."

Bingo! Abigail was getting to the bottom of things. "Oh how interesting. Tell me, how much land do you have?"

"About three acres, M'am."

"Three acres! I just sold over one hundred and fifty acres. Why, my lawn is bigger than three acres. What in the world do you call a little piece of property like that?"

Abigail was somewhat taken aback by his answer. "Well, M'am, some people call it Downtown Dallas."

My Loyal Pal

My first dog was named Colonel and I loved him more than any other animal. One Saturday morning my uncle asked me to finish the chores as he wanted to go fishing early and my reward was a forenoon off to go hiking in our woods with a city boy, Malcolm Eddy, who was visiting his grandparents on the farm next to ours. For two ten-year-old boys this would be an adventure.

It was a beautiful morning, dew on the grass and good clean smelling air in the woods. We set out to visit a cave in a rough wooded pasture when we heard a plaintive cry coming from the entrance to an abandoned fox den. At first we thought it was a baby fox but going closer we saw a timid but lonely puppy who acted as if he wanted us to go to him but kept retreating into the den. When I was able to calm him down and pick him up he began to lap my face while whining in a pitiful manner. He was obviously very hungry as well.

I surmised it was from a litter of pups whose mother had a habit of taking one or two of her brood off and abandoning them. The dog's owner, who lived about a mile in the opposite direction from our farmstead, used to sell her pups and lamented her method of family planning. We took turns carrying our rescued new friend back to the house as we wanted to get him some food as soon as possible but I dreaded having to call his owner. However, my uncle would insist that he be returned even though it would be heartbreaking for me. After drinking warm milk and having some food, the little fellow wanted to play and get acquainted with our cats that rejected him outright. Soon the man came after the pup I had already named Colonel and I refused the quarter he offered me while trying to hold back the tears. For the next two days I could think of nothing else but Colonel and finally I asked my uncle if I could buy the dog although the five dollar cost was big money at that stage of the Depression. When my uncle agreed to loan me half the price I experienced a period of panic as there was a possibility someone else had purchased the dog. When we arrived at Mr. Spriggs' place, Colonel came bounding over to the car and climbed all over me making me the happiest boy in Vermont.

When he was grown he weighed over one hundred pounds and had beautiful coloring with nicely marked medium-length brown and white hair. I moved a large packing crate to a place under the end of our long porch for his kennel where he was comfortable all year-round although if the temperature dropped much below zero he slept in the barn near the cows and with his, by now, friendly cats. He could pull me on my sled or skis so he earned a good harness to pull more effectively, although if a rabbit ran across the road through our woods he would try to follow it.

Colonel was trained not to leave the farm or cross the road but when a family moved in directly across from our place they had a large fierce dog named Bruno who would come on to our property and chase cats, cows and chickens. Colonel would chase him back but always stopped at the edge of the road as he had been trained to do. As I was walking home from school one day Bruno ran out and confronted me growling and showing his teeth. Colonel ran into the road and attacked Bruno, driving him back into his own yard. My faithful defender realized he had broken the rule and started back across the road but he was still keeping an eye on Bruno and failed to see a car speeding down the road. He was struck by the car's bumper and thrown ahead of the vehicle then was immediately run over by the front and rear wheels crushing his hind quarters. He tried to crawl towards his kennel but only reached the edge of the road so I had to help him the rest of the way. Of course it was necessary to put him down as he was in great pain and his injuries were so severe he would never be able to recover. I dwelt on my faithful, loyal and loving friend for weeks. It was a traumatic experience and I have recalled the event with great sadness many times over the years.

Mad Dog?

John Bailey looked rather down one morning. His neighbor couldn't help but notice and inquired, "John, you seem to be rather sad today. Is there something wrong you would like to talk about?"

"Well, Caleb, I had to shoot my dog this morning," responded John.

"Why, that's too bad. Was it Old Blue?"

"Ayah, Old Blue is gone."

"So tell me, John, was Old Blue mad?"

John shifted his cud of tobacco and replied, "Well, I can tell you he weren't too damned pleased about it!"

A Smart Dog

An old collie dog came with the first farm I purchased. Peggy was lazy, slept most of the time and thumped her tail for exercise. She was, however, always more alert just before meal time but promptly fell asleep as soon as she had lapped her dish clean. I discovered an amazing trait in old Peggy but wisely managed to keep it a secret for quite some time. People who visited me learned she could tell time, count and identify objects.

One evening three young ladies from town, college students, paid me a visit more to see Peggy than to enjoy my company even though I was a bachelor at the time. They soon got to the reason for coming out to the farm by asking me to demonstrate what Peggy could do, tell the time for a starter. I pointed a finger at her and said assertively, "Peggy, what time is it?" She barked her little "Woof, Woof" correctly eight times.

"Peggy, how many people are in the room?" Four, she responded. The girls were astounded. I pulled aside the curtain from the kitchen window so we could see the lighted yard where our visitors' car was parked in the snow. "Peggy, what kind of car is that? If it's a Ford bark three times, if it's an Oldsmobile bark four times and bark twice if it's a Chevrolet." Peggy barked three times and went back to lie down by the stove while the girls raved about the dog's abilities and told me to get Peggy onto the stage, to shows, even try for the movies. They were convinced I could make a fortune with the old dog and were somewhat miffed at me for my lack of interest in capitalizing on Peggy's intellect.

The trick to get Peggy to do her numbers thing was relatively simple. I'd observed that any time I pointed my finger at her and spoke rather loudly, "Peggy!" she would commence to bark, "Woof, Woof, Woof" until I dropped my finger and looked away. She would emit her little bark as long as I stared at her and kept my finger pointed in her direction. No doubt she might have made me some money before people caught on but she brought me a great deal of pleasure and Peggy thrived on the attention everyone showered on her during her last years.

Horses Remembered

Horses were always important to me. As a youth, I witnessed the transition from horses to tractors in the 1930s and early '40s. One thing that stood out in my recollections was the fact we could no longer hear the birds in the fields or much else because of the noisy tractors. Working with horses, it was necessary and humane to stop occasionally to let the horses rest or "breathe" as the old-timers used to say. The sounds were wonderful, birds singing, people's voices that carried oftentimes to the fields, and at times I used to hear the angelus from the church in a town about seven or eight miles away before the practice was done away with.

One horse I remember well could hear the bells before I did and he knew it was noon, lunch time and a respite from work in his cool stall. His teammate got the message from him and they both indicated by turning their heads toward the barn and whinnying that I should know it was quitting time. After we began to use tractors, I knew it was about noon when I saw tractors on neighboring farms heading home or perhaps a pickup truck coming out to get the workers or bring a lunch. Not being able to afford a watch, it was my habit to glance at some of the four or five adjacent farms to tell if the growling in my stomach signaled lunch time. Reflecting on the era of work horses brings back nostalgia and many fond memories as well.

Jack

When I was nine years old we acquired Black Jack, a blind horse who could fill in on odd jobs while the matched teams that worked together were used for heavier tasks. Jack trusted me, and obeyed every command, something horses that had their eyesight and were often distracted could not always be depended upon to do.

We had a one-horse wagon for various chores such as hauling firewood to storage, a one-horse hay rake, cultivators and other light equipment well-suited to a blind horse. He enjoyed being ridden and I rode him as often as my chores allowed. An example of his trust was my success in getting him to jump. I stretched a light rope across a gateway, drove him up to it till he felt it against his knees and soon got him to jump when I told him to. Jack seemed to derive as much fun as I did from his accomplishment.

Jack used to wait for me to come home from school at the corner of the pasture near the road when the weather was so he could be out. One afternoon he was not there waiting for his pat on the nose. It was a sad day, never to be forgotten, when the family broke the news that Jack was no more. Some people had blown their car's horn as they passed close to the fence and startled the poor animal. Badly frightened, he stumbled into a barbed wire fence, cut an artery and bled to death. I didn't have a horse to ride for many years after my Jack.

Robin

My father was given a small red, blind horse as a colt. She became a willing, trusting part of the family, always ready to pull a buggy in summer or a sleigh in winter. She depended on my father who cared for her with great kindness. The old barn she was sheltered in had just one large pen—the entire first floor with the hay mow above. Deep bedding kept her warm in winter and her manger was always filled with good hay. In summer she was allowed to glean the sides of the old "road" past our place as there was rarely any traffic due to the condition of the road.

For over thirty years Robin provided transportation for my father and the family and was known and admired by almost everyone except for a teenage boy who would hide in the hedgerow as my father approached and throw stones at her. The boy grew into manhood but never outgrew his cruel streak. I used to introduce him by saying, "He was a mean little cuss when he was a kid and he isn't much bigger now."

Robin's bright red coat stood out among all other horses except when my father covered her with two or three blankets while she was tied at the hitching rail in town on cold, windy days. She received many a friendly pat and kind words from passersby. When she was about thirty-five years old, grazing along the roadside, three boys came up to the fence yelling and throwing stones at her (probably cousins of that mean little cuss). She was frightened and started to run but stepped in a hole breaking her leg. She had to be put down as a broken leg in those days was a death sentence for a horse. It was almost like losing a family member.

Jake

A quite wealthy lady in town had always driven a horse and carriage but after buying her first car she wondered what to do with Jake. She hated to think of parting with her faithful steed, worrying that someone might be cruel to him. When she heard my father had lost the popular Robin, she offered him Jake but with the stipulation he must never sell the horse. My father's reputation for being kind to animals left the lady with great peace of mind. When it was time to take the horse home my father started to lead him out of the barn.

"Wait," said the lady. "Put his harness on him and all the other things you can use." After harnessing Jake my Dad started to leave again but was told he needed to take her carriage as well.

"I won't need it and people aren't buying horse-drawn equipment any more so take it and use it. It's just taking up room in the barn. I know you will take good care of Jake."

My father was very pleased and enjoyed driving through town and up the highway in style. Jake's last several years were much more enjoyable than most horses of those times.

Old Bill

My uncle acquired a horse that no one had been able to break, a wild three-year-old mustang with a mind of his own and boundless energy. My father was called upon to try to make the beast at least safe to be around but my father, in spite of his skill with horses, declared Old Bill could never be trained to work well with another horse to make a team. My uncle put him to work matched up with a very large horse hoping to tire out the wild mustang. Bill pranced and banged his head against his teammate, tried to gallop if headed in the direction of the barn but dragged his feet if turned back to the work at hand. He refused to obey commands. Everyone wondered why my uncle put up with him but he kept the unruly animal for more than thirty years, during which time Old Bill wore out more than a dozen teammates.

When I tried to lead him out to the watering trough twice a day, he led me. He would leap into the air, kick his heels before landing but never kicked me but once and that was after five years of my struggling with him. When Bill was about fifteen years old he survived a terrible accident. The horse stables were, at that time, on the second floor of the barn directly over one row of cows in their stanchions. One night the plank floor of Bill's stall gave way and his rear quarters dropped down into the cow stable. His halter held him from falling all the way so his hind legs were dangling through the hole in the floor while much of his weight was held by the halter, obviously causing great discomfort. The jagged, broken planks cut into his body at the juncture of his legs, made worse by his struggles, while the steel horseshoes on his hoofs severely injured the cow directly below him. The poor animal apparently had hung in that painful, awkward position for several hours before my uncle came into the barn at 4 a.m. to milk his cows. A hired man said he heard a noise about midnight but he didn't investigate. It was a difficult rescue operation as the 1,600 pound horse had to be lifted with block and tackle and moved to a suitable location to recover from his injuries.

With a lot of attention and veterinary care Old Bill recovered after several weeks, badly scarred, but was soon jumping around and playing his old tricks. He lived to work another 15 years demonstrating how durable and tough he was.

One Sunday morning when I was eighteen years old, I was about to release him to go to the horse pasture across the barnyard. He bit my wrist, smashing my new watch (a graduation gift), then ran kicking and jumping down to the cow pasture gate which had been negligently left open just enough so he could get a start through before breaking the gate. He ran about twenty feet to a small stone pile where he stumbled and flopped over onto his back breaking his hind leg.

My uncle moved him into the shade of a toolshed and sat all day with him before putting him out of his misery. One might think my uncle would be relieved at his passing but perhaps they both shared a stubborn streak. Usually a dead farm animal would be taken off to a rendering plant to end up as fertilizer but my uncle drew Old Bill to a remote corner of the farm and buried him by hand—no small task. So ended the thirty-year love-hate relationship.

Bill, Not to Be Confused with Old Bill

We needed an extra horse after losing Jack. Bill, also blind, was heavier, stronger and was a dark bay color in contrast to Black Jack. This animal was a delight to work with and seemed to enjoy being out in the fields no matter what the weather or the kind of work he was put to. We never paired him up to work with Old Bill, not only because of Old Bill's temperament but also because horses respond to their names and two Bills together would be very confusing to them.

Bill was an honest worker and was rewarded in several ways. He had more time off and quite often I would slip him an apple or a carrot. In the fall we usually turned the horses into a large meadow where the feed was very good and they could relax. Bill always came up with the other horses when they came to drink at a water tank near the barn. One evening we noticed Bill hadn't followed the others and we thought perhaps he didn't want to leave the lush forage of the meadow. We kept the horses in a small pasture near the barn during the night and I was very concerned about Bill even though he never panicked and could usually find his way home.

There was a dance that evening and I decided to go but kept thinking of Bill so around midnight when I came home I drove over to the meadow to look for him. My headlights showed a broken gate that led to a pasture and a twenty-acre woodlot on the back side of the large meadow. After parking the car, I took a flashlight and could see the marks of horse shoes leading beyond the gate. The tracks then led across the pasture along a farm road that led to and through the woods. Bill must have been able to follow the road until it came to a gate that allowed us to enter our neighbor's land to go around a very steep wooded cliff to our fields down below. This gate was also broken and the tracks showed poor Bill had become frightened and had started to run down across some very rough, steep, rocky terrain. At one point he had fallen but then continued downhill towards the cliff which was at least forty feet high and vertical. He had run at a gallop to the precipice and by the light of my flashlight I saw the fresh scrape marks his shoes had made on the bare rock that formed the cliff. He had fallen straight down landing on his back and was wedged between the base of the rock wall and a large tree. His eyes were wide open but he must have died instantly.

It was a ghastly sight but there was nothing to be done at one o'clock in the morning. Sadly, after Sunday mass it was my task to go down and remove his shoes and halter. His bones were still around the base of the same tree forty years later.

Dan, the Circus Horse

We learned the history of this horse after noticing he responded to music in a strange way. One Memorial Day I was planting corn when the local school started its march to the cemetery behind a band that carried quite loudly the half mile to the cornfield. Dan became very excited, whinnied and pranced along with his head turned toward the music. His former owner told us Dan had been with a circus and when the business downsized he was sold. The music must have reminded him of his years in the circus.

Dan worked on the farm while I was away in the service but was sold at auction when my uncle had to sell out due to his health. The sad part was no one knew who bought him and the new owner did not ask the horse's name. It was always difficult for a horse to have new owners and have to learn a new name.

Kate

A huge strawberry roan named Kate was the meanest horse I ever saw. My uncle may have bought her to help keep Old Bill in line because she would bite Bill when he banged his head against her as he always tried to do to his other teammates. Kate would sometimes crowd anyone against the side of her stall as they tried to enter to put on her bridle. She would kick without provocation and was very stubborn about pulling her share of the load. People said her former owner had named her after his first wife. She finally proved to be unmanageable and Old Bill who had worn out more than a dozen good horses started to balk at being hitched up with her. Kate's reputation made her unsaleable to most farmers but one man named Jenkins came along and said he could tame her but even he could not change her mean streak. Another horse-knowledgeable individual told Jenkins how to cure her. "I have encountered this trait in horses many times and I have the solution. Put an ounce of lead in her right ear."

"OK," said Jenkins, "But how do I put the lead in her ear?"

"With a gun," was the reply.

Big Dan

We bought another horse named Dan, a huge animal whose health was grossly misrepresented to us. This was not an unusual occurrence in horse trading transactions of those days but that didn't make it acceptable, nor was it often possible to get one's money back. It was buyer beware. The previous owner had insisted on having his hired man deliver Dan by riding him horseback the eight or nine miles to our place. I had looked forward to having that long ride myself. Dan was the largest horse we ever had and was very gentle but the first time we put him to work he started "heaving." Heaves was the term for a severe respiratory disorder that caused the animal to have such trouble trying to breathe he had to stop and gasp for breath. Dusty conditions exacerbated the condition.

Apparently the hired man had allowed Dan to rest frequently on the way to catch his breath so as not to have him arrive showing any signs of distress. Legally the man could have been sued for selling a horse unable to work but my uncle never had a lawsuit in his life and accepted his loss quietly and was glad he hadn't paid a big price. When we replaced him we found a good home for him on a small farm owned by an older couple who only needed a horse to do minimal work around the place. The old gentleman took care of him for many years. He had a large box stall to himself and could go out to a small pasture whenever he pleased. It was horse heaven where he was more of a pet than a beast of burden.

Not Funny

After the great hurricane of 1950 I started a year-long operation to salvage what was left of a stand of spruce on one of my woodlots some distance from home. Almost every tree was either broken off or tipped over so it was necessary to take out each tree and decide what portion could be saved for useful timber. I hired a man with a good team of horses to skid the logs out of the woods to an open meadow where we could work more efficiently.

The horses were so well trained that while one horse would draw out a log to where a man would unhook the load, the second horse would be going back for another log. This made for a very efficient operation, one horse going while the other was coming back. It only required a man at each end to manage the horses while two of us cut the broken trees into sections.

The man who owned the horses shocked me when we finished our operation in the woodlot. After I paid him and started to gather up my tools, he turned to one side and shot both horses dead in their tracks. As I stared in disbelief the man announced he had no more work for the horses and didn't want to feed them any longer. I would have gladly bought the pair of wonderful, faithful animals had I known how little he appreciated them. Their bones lay at the edge of the woods for many years, a stark reminder of how callous some people are.

Dan and Dolly, and Mark and Jessie

Four Percheron horses came with my first farm. Dan and Dolly made up a well-matched team and worked every day as the prime power in the fields and woodlots. In the early spring they pulled the "sap sled" from the woods to the sugarhouse where maple syrup was made. They usually started in deep snow and by the time the sugaring season was over they struggled through deep mud. Dan and Dolly were registered Percherons with typical mottled gray color, while Mark and Jessie, Dolly's offspring, were coal black, suggesting that perhaps Dolly had crossed the color line at least twice.

The older of the two colts was quite dangerous. She would come at a person on her hind legs while she struck out with her front feet as if she meant to kill anyone who might try to tame her. I had neither the time nor the finesse to train her but my seventy-six-year-old father had a way with horses and when he was visiting me at the farm he was appalled that no one had broken this wild filly. He directed us to get her into a stall and put a harness on her. This was no small task but at considerable risk, not to her, we managed to get her harnessed and somewhat subdued. After a struggle we followed my father's directions and hitched her up with her mother to the front half of a sled although there was no snow on the ground. With much bucking and kicking the filly soon settled down with her mother, and my father managed to drive them around a small field.

We could never get the wild critter harnessed again but a man came and offered to buy the two colts. He was a professional horse trainer but I never learned what success he had although the younger male colt was much more tractable and no doubt submitted to training. The filly may have been served up as "horse burgers."

No Compassion

Growing up in the era when horses were beasts of burden, it has always been appalling to me how men of those times could be so cruel and neglectful of those wonderful creatures. They were literally slaves who had to learn commands, to be ready for work at any time and endure the heat and cold of the seasons. They were often fed poor quality feed. In Vermont it was a common practice to give the horses the hay left over in the cows' mangers as well as the least expensive grain. Quite often they lived their entire working lives without a bit of change in diet. As a small boy I often tried to take an apple, a carrot or anything for a little variety to them and it brought me pleasure to see how they relished even a morsel.

While working in crops such as corn, most farmers placed a wire guard over the horse's nose and mouth to prevent him from grabbing a bite of the fresh smelling corn. Other farmers made use of the check rein, a strap that was attached to each end of the bit in the horse's mouth and was looped up around the hames, rigid protuberances above the collar. This method kept the horse from reaching down to sample a bit of the crop but also held the head too high, in a very uncomfortable position. It was natural for horses to be able to lower their heads in order to pull efficiently.

There were hundreds of ways the poor beasts suffered because owners failed to adjust or oil harnesses to make them more comfortable. Many were watered only twice a day even in the summer heat. After a hard day's work during the hot haying season, sweat and dirt left a crust of dry material that needed washing off, followed by a good brushing for the animal to get a decent night's rest. It was enjoyable for me to slosh pails of water over their bodies and squeegee it off afterwards with a stiff brush. At an early age I developed the habit of lifting parts of the harness during a rest stop to allow air to circulate and cool those areas where the straps of the harness chafed the most.

Another unnecessary device was the use of bridles with blinders. A horse's eyes are placed to enable them to see more to the side but their forward vision was restricted as well by blinders. They worked their lives out being able to see only the inside of the leather contraptions. When I owned work horses of my own I removed those torturous additions to the bridle. They seemed much more at ease not having to guess what was going on each side of them.

I sometimes long for those days of working with horses but now when I reflect on the miserable existence they led and the cruel neglect some of them suffered, it's a comfort to realize it was a blessing when tractors took over the heavy work on the farm. The revival of interest in horses for pleasure today has resulted in much more kindness towards these remarkable and beautiful creatures.

Say That Again?

When I first entered the service, field grade officers were mounted for parades which usually took place on Saturdays. One colonel I thought was quite picky about his steed but he heard I was from a farm in Vermont so wanted me to take care of his horse. He called me in one morning and said, "Angier, take my horse out and have it shod." He was from the Deep South and I had difficulty understanding him but we had been drilled to carry out an order immediately and never question an order. However, wondering why he would have such a magnificent animal "shot," I decided to delay carrying out this order. It is well I did for when I pretended to have done the deed and went in to ask the colonel, "Sir, where do you want the horse buried?" he of course exploded and only my hasty departure out the door on the run saved me from bodily harm.

The old sergeant who had primary care of all the horses managed to calm the colonel down and explained how I had misunderstood him but didn't have the heart to put such a nice animal down. The next day the colonel's horse had the new shoes and I had KP—peeling potatoes, scrubbing pots and carrying out garbage for a week.

Say What?

After World War II horses were not in demand and farmers often gave them away as they converted to tractors. One enterprising old codger went around the county offering to take "that old horse off your hands." When deer hunting season came around he put his free animals in the remote fields and woods of his poor but quite extensive acreage and charged a fee for down-country hunters.

Three very inexperienced men from the city paid for the privilege of possibly getting a deer or perhaps three deer and started up into the back country of the farm. After hunting all day they came out of the woods dead tired and started across a field. One of them saw an old horse and shouted, "There's a deer!" All three fired their rifles and the horse went down riddled with bullets. As the excited hunters ran to the poor beast, one of the men said, "I never thought deer were such big animals!"

"Yes, and look at the size of his feet, gigantic!" said one of his companions. "Wait a minute" said the third man. "Look here, this SOB is wearing shoes! I think we have killed a horse!"

About this time the old farmer, hearing the shots, came steaming up the hill towards the hunters gathered around the horse. "What have you done? You've killed my horse!" he panted.

The three men were now quite frightened. "We will pay for it. We will pay for it!" they shouted in unison.

"Pay for it? I guess you will pay for it! That horse was worth $25,000 dollars!"

One of the guilty hunters stammered, "How could it be worth all that money?"

"You fools," the angry old man said. "You are supposed to look before you shoot. That wonderful animal could communicate in four languages!"

As they stood aghast, one of the men spoke up and asked, "If that is true, then why didn't he say something?"

Poor Woman!

Officers in the National Guard, along with career men in other branches of the military, were required to attend various schools if they were serious about advancement. When I attended a course at Fort Benning, Georgia, most of my fellow classmen were admonished by their commanding officers to come back in the top ten percent of the class or forget about any promotions in their lifetimes. These young men worked desperately hard and some of them were generals several years later commanding forces in Viet Nam and in the Persian Gulf. Some became "Chairbourne" Generals in the Pentagon.

I had no such ambitions and very little interest in military affairs except subjects that applied to my field of aviation. In a large room holding about three hundred men we listened to lectures and heard discourses on personal experiences in command situations. If an officer wanted to speak or comment on the issue being presented he needed to raise his arm and an enlisted man would run to him with a microphone on a long cord. One mouthy captain with shiny new bars reveled in holding forth on his favorite subject: training. He complained about the new second lieutenants that were sent to him poorly trained, incompetent and quite useless to him. The new captain droned on complaining about those "shavetails" the training camps were turning out.

When he finally finished I raised my arm and for the first time at the school spoke to the other officers in the class. I requested a moment of silence out of respect for his mother and to meditate on what she went through when he was born with those captain's bars on his shoulders. He had obviously forgotten he was once a second lieutenant himself. My remarks made me some points with the rest of the class and brought a little levity into the room. Nevertheless, while most of the others struggled to end up in the top ten percent I ended up in the *bottom* ten percent.

Will it Ever End?

As prisoners of war in a Nazi prison in Poland, we frequently speculated on when the war would end and what our fate might be when that time came. Our captors had several options: exterminate us, keep us as human shields when the allies approached or peacefully return us to Allied control.

Several slogans made the rounds as to our future:
"Home alive in '45"
"Out of this fix in '46
"Home or heaven in '47"
"Golden Gate in '48"
"Will my wife still be mine in '49?"

"Won't it be nifty in 1950?

Other slogans were passed around but these I remember most clearly. It was a chancy time for young men in confinement and most of us still living give thanks every morning for our deliverance.

A Close Shave

A man in the next town bought and sold horses, often having fifteen or twenty on hand at a time. He was very unpopular because he allowed his herd to wander quite freely, finding feed in farmers' fields in summer and eating out of their haystacks in the winter. When I was three years old we lived on a side road that hardly anyone ever traveled so it was not usually very dangerous for us children to play in the road. My siblings were at school one day when I found it great fun to float an oblong, boat-shaped, tin can down the small ditch beside the road. After placing the can in the water I would run alongside to the end of our yard. Wondering how much load the makeshift boat could carry, I was putting dirt from the road into the can when I felt the ground shake and a loud rumbling noise behind me. My mother heard the sound and started towards me but instantly we both saw what looked like a disaster in the making. The renegade horses were not more than fifty feet from me and running at full speed down the road. Before I could move, their legs were flashing past me and over me while I disappeared from my mother's view in the dust. More than a dozen horses went over me but not one hoof struck me and it all happened so quickly I couldn't have moved if I'd tried.

My mother slumped to the ground no doubt certain she would find only my trampled body when the dust cleared. It was the first of many close brushes with death I was to experience in life.

"Dan" & "Bill" hitched to new cultivator.
Horse passing by was Deacon Jones who
carried school children.

My father Frank Xavier Angier
1871-1949
Maried Mamie Odette
February 1906

1928
Francis Angier, age 5
age of fish unknown but he was heavy.

1928 Francis age 5
At Long Point Lake Champlain just north of Basin Habor.

July 1928
Francis age 5 with last load of wood from a pile moved into
a shed under the barn over a period of 2 months for $4.00

1930 age 7
with "Jack Dempsey" had his legs
cut off by a mowing machine. He
crawled under a barn and died.

Big "Dan"

1934
Francis and "Colonel"
age 11   age 5 month

"Black Jack" a blind horse.
I taught him to jump.

My uncle and two younger brothers haying 1943.
"Dolly" and "Dan the circus horse"

Last visit with my uncle Byron Clark before leaving for overseas.

Jan, 4 1947
Madeleine and Francis Angier
Wedding Day

July 1950
Barn built in 1948 one of four barns built on two
farms in Addison.
Madeleine Angier and John Francis Jr. 1 year old.

J. F. Angier, with T-33, Vermont Air National Guard, Burlington, VT 1955

GRAND PARENTS HOMESTEAD, PHOTO TAKIN IN 1904, IN NEW HAVEN MILLS VERMONT.
Left to right are: Ella Angier - Emma Angier (my aunts) - Elmira Cadieux Angier, Grand mother - Julia Cadieux Angier, Great grand mother (she lived to be 103 years old) - Frank Xavier Angier, my father - Joseph Angier, my uncle.

Francis' Home
The connected buildings on the farm in New Haven, Vermont where I was brought up. Fire destroyed this complex during a severe storm in 1938. The house, built in 1796, was very large, and connected to a three story building that, in turn, attached to a large barn.

The Gypsies

Gypsy caravans used to go by our house at least once every summer on the nearly abandoned road to a field to camp about a half-mile from our house. While they were in the area everyone guarded their horses as in those days gypsies were thought to steal any horses they could get to. My father would sit up or sleep in the barn until they broke camp and left.

At four years old I thought the colorful wagons (forerunners of our present day RVs) were exciting and the women with painted faces who peered out of the small windows of the vans often waved and smiled. In the evenings we could hear the music and see the bonfires as these strange people entertained themselves. One day the attraction was too much for me so I walked down the roadway and turned off to the campground to see things at close range. They answered my many questions patiently and allowed me to look inside the wagons. Meanwhile, my father and mother began to miss me but thought perhaps I had gone to the neighbors with my older brother to play.

Towards darkness my brother had come home and a serious search was started for me. Meanwhile, the gypsies began to feel I had overstayed my visit and when I pointed out my house to them, across the fields, about four men and boys started walking me home. They encountered my father and siblings looking for me who were very relieved and were even more surprised the gypsies had not kept me as it was rumored they often "adopted" children. All of my father's concern for having his horse stolen was for naught because my hosts, for the day, broke tradition and gave my father a horse! It could be that I had made such a nuisance of myself that they thought my father needed to be rewarded for putting up with me. I thought this band of gypsies was kind, generous and didn't seem to be the sort who would steal horses or children.

Note: My father was diplomatic enough to not refuse the gift horse outright but explained he didn't need an extra horse and could not afford to feed another one but was willing to sell him back to them for a dollar.

John, the Hired Man

About every two weeks we used to take grain to a mill near the railroad station to be ground and have other grain mixed with it for cow feed. I was always eager to go because the mill had a delightful odor about it, trains came and went at the "Junction" as it was called and there were usually some interesting happenings. The leisurely trip on the farm wagon was a real treat for me at age five.

On one excursion, some hobos alighted from a freight train and one of them approached my uncle and asked for a job. Usually he would have been turned down but this young man was clean cut, handsome and had a winning personality. He carried his only possessions in a green bag which we later found contained a clean shirt, underwear, socks and a razor. He introduced himself as John and said he would work for room and board and not be any trouble. My uncle didn't need more help at the time but agreed to try it thinking he might get some things done around the farmstead that had been put off.

John sat near me on the bags of grain as we rode home and talked about many things. We saw a piece of history as we traveled parallel to some railroad tracks and saw a train making its last trip to Bristol, a short run of about six miles. The railroad company was losing money and the Great Depression was just beginning so the short line was closed down and the tracks taken up. It used to make two or three stops for passengers between the two terminals and was famous for the locomotive's design. It pulled the cars going up to Bristol and pushed them on the way back. Once a year it was brought to the Junction to be turned around on a turntable. Its lonesome whistle was fondly called the "Bristol Bellyache" and we missed its mournful sound especially at night. Because of his obvious interest in railroads, I told John all I knew about the small rail line.

My aunt was somewhat apprehensive about having a stranger in the house but she was soon delighted when John willingly helped her wash windows, mop the floor or lightened her workload in his spare time. He adapted to the routine quickly, performed each task to perfection and did it all cheerfully.

I followed him about, listening to his comments, laughing at his stories and all the while learning how to do things. He washed his meager wardrobe himself and always appeared clean no matter what he worked at. He had many talents and helped my uncle to the extent he received more than the room and board he had asked for—a few dollars a week. I really loved him and he was my best friend all summer.

The family used to go to Bristol or Vergennes to do the weekly shopping but John only went if we were going to Vergennes. Some years later it occurred to me that he might have gone to Vergennes because it had a railroad station. On his last trip with us he didn't show up for the ride home. After waiting and driving around looking for him, we gave up and we never saw John again. He probably hopped onto a freight train and it was obvious he had planned to leave as I could not find his green bag in his room. He was clever enough to stash his few belongings someplace in the car where we wouldn't see it. It was a devastating happening for me and I shed many tears that summer and have thought about John many times over the years.

Whenever I think of John, who worked for us that long ago summer, the memories of the hardships of those times come back.

John was classed as a "hobo" but he was honest and we all hoped he prospered and the time came when he no longer had to ride the railroad cars around the country looking for work.

Prohibition and the Depression

This is a good place to record some of the happenings during this period of history when good men had to become hobos to survive and families had to beg on the streets.

There were some opportunists who made fortunes during Prohibition and strangely, many more who became very wealthy even in the Depression years that followed. However, most of these business ventures were exploitive of the victims of those times. We will take Charlie (a real person) for an example and how he climbed upward on the backs of the most destitute families.

Charlie made his first money as a bootlegger. He prospered, paid for his large farm and placed his money in secure places that weathered the stock market crash of 1929. Banks began calling in loans on homes and farms and farm families took the brunt of the catastrophic events that occurred during the early 1930s. Most were dairy farmers who depended on the sale of milk to stay in business but the price of milk dropped to less than a dollar a hundred pounds. The most frugal families had been just getting by on $3 a hundred while the mortgage payments stayed the same. If a farmer tried to meet his expenses and payments by selling a cow or two the result was devastating because no one had money to buy them. Cows that would have sold for $50 to $150 brought as little as $4 to $12. For Charlie, this opened up a ripe and fertile field for harvesting.

With his valuable debt-free farm as security he had no trouble borrowing a few thousand dollars to start purchasing farms on the verge of foreclosure. He had no compassion for the families on those farms and never paid a penny more than the amount they owed the bank.

Remember, the family's home was part of the farm so it was a wrenching episode in their lives to be put out on the road with only their meager belongings.

Charlie even took advantage of their terrible state by offering them the use of the house in return for working the farm for him at starvation wages. A laborer could earn a dollar a day and had to furnish his own living quarters as well as feed his family. Amazingly, many desperately poor people did just that. Those families who chose to remain on the farm all worked harder than ever to earn eight or ten dollars a week. Charlie made sure every stall in each barn was occupied by one of the $6 or $8 cows. He wanted each of his tenant farmers and their families to be working every hour of every day.

The ten-gallon cans of milk had to be at the roadside early in the morning to be picked up by one of Charlie's trucks. This was usually not later than 6 A.M so chores had to be under way by about 4 a.m. Unless his tenant farmers had hay to put in or crops to plant Charlie picked them up to work on his own farm where he raised many acres of vegetables, most of which were sold to stores and only small quantities were left to his workers' families. He carried the vegetable business a step further by getting the tenants' wives to can and pickle some of the produce to be sold, leaving them only a small amount in pay for their labor.

Charlie began to offer some of his best workers the opportunity to purchase a farm but wrote the contracts so they could never finish paying the mortgage. A few of these families put their heart and soul into managing the farm, improving the buildings, fences and general appearance of the place. Children worked to feed calves to replace older cows or some who did not produce a fair amount of milk. After a few years when Charlie could see how much more valuable the farm had become, he would start proceedings to take the property back. He had written a provision into the mortgage allowing him to demand payment in full at his discretion putting the family through another ordeal of eviction or becoming vassals again.

Fortunately, times began to get better as the economy revived, milk prices improved and real estate became more valuable again. Some of the more sharp-minded farmers realized they could keep their farms by refinancing with a bank. A farm with a mortgage of $8,000 could be appraised for possibly $12,000, leaving equity large enough for the down payment. Federal legislation was also passed to provide loans at low interest over a term of forty years. Charlie had made his millions during the worst economic period of our history but failed in his attempts to satisfy the IRS and spent some time in prison.

A Fishing Trip

It was a great treat for me to go fishing with my uncle and I also enjoyed the company of "Uncle Sam," an old English gentleman who boarded with the family. One day Uncle Birchard, known as "Birch," also went with us. It was a rare day that my uncle ever came home without a good catch of fish. He would clean them and drop off fish to friends and relatives along the way home but this day was different. The fish had more patience than we did so when we arrived home nearly empty-handed, my aunt made fun of us until I told her we did bring home something. I related how "Uncle Sam caught a clam and Uncle Birch caught a perch." Pretty good for a six-year-old poet.

Mary Jane and Epitaphs

From the time I was nine years old until the "big trouble" called World War II my spare time was spent working in a cemetery. Whenever my presence was not needed on the family farm, one could find my bike parked against the iron fence in front of Evergreen Cemetery. Pushing a lawn mower among the tombstones developed more than powerful muscles; I soon learned to read the epitaphs on the go, so to speak, and after a time knew many of them by heart.

My interest in this part of American life and death remained with me over the years and quite often old New England cemeteries provide me with quiet relaxation and entertainment. Epitaphs range from funny through sad, to tragic. There are inscriptions that evoke mystery, lightly concealed resentment and dual meaning. Quite often the old words chiseled in stone inspire the reader to investigate the story of the person for whom those words are written.

The words on Mary Jane's headstone motivated me to do considerable research that developed a tale of excitement and pity concerning a woman who possessed charm and wit but lacked good judgment. Mary Jane, I learned, was a coquette, a temptress and a professional tease. Teasing was not only her greatest pleasure and sport but became a way of life.

She flirted and teased at work as well as at parties and dances. In the late '20s and early '30s, she dressed in a provocative style for the times and had great fun leading men on only to leave them frustrated after an evening of amorous expectation. My probing of Mary Jane's life made me wonder how she escaped bodily harm through all her years of tempting so many men to her door, a door so often slammed shut in their faces. Scientists say no energy expended is ever really lost and in Mary Jane's case this was certainly true in regard to the girls who knew her well. The other girls often capitalized on her "rebounds," the frustrated escorts Mary Jane laughed at from behind her door. Other girls grabbed them up before the treatment wore off and one in particular who lived next door used to slip into the man's car to exploit to its fullest his mood of the moment.

As Mary Jane grew older and wiser she tried to taper off her role as a coquette but her reputation was fixed and clung to her like a shadow. By the 1940s she became more alarmed and was haunted by the thought of going through life as a spinster. Plainly she had overdone the tease routine by about fifteen years. No man she had trifled with would swallow his pride and women who knew her were of no help, especially since in wartime a good man was hard to find.

Life was passing her by and her desperate search for a man came to no avail. It was as if her reputation as a tease had formed a force field about her to the extent that even a stranger sensed trouble in any association with her. Truly, she was being punished severely for her past escapades in which she had taken such pleasure and delight. What had been fun in her younger years had become a millstone around her neck.

By the 1950s she was a pathetic figure as she wandered about with a desperate, haunted look. She took to frequenting post office lobbies to scrutinize the wanted posters, sometimes offering five hundred dollars more than the government for the apprehension of a fugitive.

In spite of all her efforts to convince people she had reformed, poor Mary Jane died a frustrated old maid. Her few relatives wanted to do something for her but were left with limited funds after her last years of care and burial expenses. Fortunately, her cousin Sadie knew a newspaperman who agreed to write an appropriate epitaph on her simple headstone. The family was not aware he was a sportswriter so they were somewhat startled to read his contribution permanently engraved in marble.

HERE LIES MARY JANE
FOR WHOM LIFE HAD NO TERRORS
FOR HER LIFE WAS VERY PLAIN
NO HITS NO RUNS NO ERRORS

Riley

One inscription on a stone was not hard to figure out. It seems that one Brian Le May had an ongoing amorous affair with the wife of the local barber, Howard Riley. Brian decided to spend a night with his lover while Riley was attending a convention in a city some distance away. However, Riley had become suspicious and decided to return home a day early. He saw Le May's car parked near the Riley residence so decided to maintain a surveillance until Brian came out and drove away in his Model "A" Ford.

The two men had always been good friends and shared many a drink together so their acquaintances never suspected anything sinister had taken place between them. The Rileys lived a somewhat more lavish lifestyle because of his prosperous barbershop while Le May's income made it impossible to even approach his friend's more satisfying activities. He spent money he didn't have.

The barber kept quiet about his discovery until Brian came in for a shave and haircut. Something distracted Riley, so the story goes, and the razor slipped, severing Brian's carotid artery. Now Brian Le May was a gregarious person, always playing tricks and joking, well-liked by many but still he had that habit of living beyond his means. The term used in those times for a high living person was "living the life of Riley" but no one made the connection in this particular case.

Once the neighborhood recovered from the tragedy, there was an outpouring of sympathy and generous actions that made Brian's widow grateful and thankful for the support. The barber joined in with an offer to pay for the popular victim's memorial inasmuch as the accident happened in his shop. The epitaph tells more of the story but could be construed to be somewhat ambivalent.

HERE LIES BRIAN LE MAY
WHO WAS HUMOROUS AND WILEY
HE TRIED TO LIVE THE LIFE OF RILEY
WHILE RILEY WAS AWAY

Others I remember:

Beneath this stone lies Bridget Ormsby
Talked herself to death at her bridge club

I love this cheerful spot
It's not a place of gloom
Because it's my husband's tomb

A lonely life I've lived and sad
The marriage knot was never tied
And I wish my father never had

Here lies Amos Pope
Who stole a horse and died on a rope

There was a man over in the middle of Vermont who didn't get along with people so they buried him outside the gate of the cemetery.

A couple was walking in the cemetery when they encountered a woman lying on the ground in front of a headstone crying, pounding on the turf and wailing, "Why did you have to die, why?" The couple was moved with compassion for the woman and asked if it was her husband's grave. "No, no!" she sobbed. "This is his first wife's grave!"

You Tell Him!

Reginald won a little money at the race track and felt like treating himself to something special. He entered a swank beauty parlor and ordered "the works"—haircut, facial, pedicure, manicure. After a lot of attention by the staff he became a little bold and spoke to the nice-looking woman who was doing his nails. "How about stepping out with me this evening? We can have dinner, have a few drinks and who knows what later."

Without looking up, she answered, "I can't. I'm married."

Still feeling adventurous, Reg suggested, "Just tell your husband you are going out with your girlfriend."

"Tell him yourself, he's shaving you."

Mrs. God?

Back in the 1970s, I was asked to speak at Windham College down in the southeastern part of Vermont. My topic was to be about organic farming and the "appropriate technology" people getting into farming might need to acquire. Of course, it was necessary for me to wait my turn while the other speakers delivered inspiring and very professional presentations. There seemed, however, to be a theme running through all the talks of a "hippie" philosophy that was somewhat alien to me. The woman who introduced me was an ardent feminist and had made attempts to get the idea across that God is a woman. The last words of her introduction were,

"Mr. Angier, don't you agree since we always refer to 'Mother Nature' that God must be a woman?"

By the time I was able to get to the podium and adjust the microphone, an appropriate answer had come to me. "Your belief may be unpopular, Madame, but not without merit. I have it on good authority that God is indeed a woman."

"Oh how exciting! And may I ask who or what was your reliable source?" she wanted to know.

"The devil herself told me and I try never to argue with a woman."

There was plenty of time for me to get my notes together before the applause and some half-hearted boos died down.

So That's Why!

Here is a question: Why didn't Eve help Adam in the Garden of Eden? Well, she was too busy raising Cain.

God's Pharmacy

It's been said that God first separated the salt water from the fresh, made dry land, planted a garden, made animals and fish...all before making a human. He made and provided what we'd need before we were born. These are best and more powerful when eaten raw. We're such slow learners.... God left us a great clue as to what foods help what part of our body! God's Pharmacy! Amazing!

A sliced carrot looks like the human eye. The pupil, iris and radiating lines look just like the human eye... and YES, science now shows carrots greatly enhance blood flow to and function of the eyes.

A tomato has four chambers and is red. The heart has four chambers and is red. All of the research shows tomatoes are loaded with lycopine and are indeed pure heart and blood food.

Grapes hang in a cluster that has the shape of the heart. Each grape looks like a blood cell and all of the research today shows grapes are also profound heart and blood vitalizing food.

A walnut looks like a little brain, a left and right hemisphere, upper cerebrums and lower cerebrums. Even the wrinkles or folds on the nut are just like the neo-cortex. We now know walnuts help develop more than three dozen neuron-transmitters for brain function.

Kidney beans actually heal and help maintain kidney function and yes, they look exactly like the human kidneys.

Celery, bok choy, rhubarb and many more look just like bones. These foods specifically target bone strength. Bones are 23% sodium and these foods are 23% sodium. If you don't have enough sodium in your diet, the body pulls it from the bones, thus making them weak. These foods replenish the skeletal needs of the body.

Avocadoes, eggplant and pears target the health and function of the womb and cervix of the female?they look just like these organs. Today's research shows that when a woman eats one avocado a week, it balances hormones, sheds unwanted birth weight, and prevents cervical cancers. And how profound is this? It takes exactly nine months to grow an avocado from blossom to ripened fruit. There are over 14,000 photolytic chemical constituents of nutrition in each one of these foods (modern science has only studied and named about 141 of them).

Figs are full of seeds and hang in twos when they grow. Figs increase the mobility of male sperm and increase the numbers of sperm as well as overcome male sterility.

Sweet potatoes look like the pancreas and actually balance the glycemic index of diabetics.

Olives assist the health and function of the ovaries.

Oranges, grapefruit, and other citrus fruits look just like the mammary glands of the female and actually assist the health of the breasts and the movement of lymph in and out of the breasts.

Onions look like the body's cells. Today's research shows onions help clear waste materials from all of the body's cells. They even produce tears that wash the epithelial layers of the eyes.

A working companion of the onion, garlic, also helps eliminate waste materials and dangerous free radicals from the body.

Note: These observations have intrigued me for many years and seem logical. Natural health and nutrition have always been of great interest to me.

Father Liddy

As young people we thought our beloved priest would be with us forever but the bishop decided to rotate the pastors around the state and we heard Father Liddy would be leaving us. The ladies of the parish went all out to give him a proper farewell party. It was a really nice affair but of course it was a sad occasion as well. I particularly liked the refreshments myself. One fond memory I have of his jovial nature was how he greeted my grandmother when she came for confession to make her Easter Duties. He made it a pleasant affair and heard her confession on his back lawn as they walked back and forth.

Finally it was time to say goodbye. Everyone joined the long line to speak their last words to the popular priest and shake his hand. Just ahead of me was Mrs. Davy who was so upset she broke down just as she shook his hand. Father comforted her as best he could, saying, "Now, now, my dear lady, don't take it so hard, you will soon have a new priest and you will come to love him, too." "Oh, no, Father, that's the trouble, they get worse all the time!"

At Church

The preacher was really wound up on his sermon about sin. After covering all the bases and then some he looked over the congregation and asked, "Is there anyone here who can honestly say he likes sin?" Fred Thomas stood up. Everyone gasped and turned to look at Fred. When the minister recovered his wits he asked, "Sir, do you honestly admit that you like sin?"

"Oh, excuse me, Preacher, I thought you said gin."

The ladies of the local church put on great dinners on Town Meeting Day. The pastor was a very strict but personable lady but unfortunately had lived a life devoid of humor and could never get the point of a funny story. As I started to dip into a huge bowl of punch she was guarding, the devil in me told me to get her to smile so I asked politely if the punch was "spiked." That began a forceful discourse on the evils of alcohol directed at me eye to eye. I was somewhat taken aback by the intensity of her remarks and, because she had raised her voice, several other people began to listen to her lecture to me. "I have never touched a drop of alcohol in my life," she announced. "I never drink anything but pure water and we travel all the way up to the town where we used to live and get our water from the spring there."

I had spilled some of my punch on the table because of her direct dressing down all aimed at me and was wiping up some of it with a napkin while trying to think of something to say. Finally it came to me. "Yes, of course, I know that spring. Very popular. People go there and drink gallons of it although I don't care for it myself and have never had any more than the first sip. Yes, that famous spring is just below the big distillery up there." She still didn't smile but the listeners had a good laugh. I explained to her that I was not addicted to drink but rather addicted to crude jokes at times.

She accepted my apology and before she moved away I managed to get a smile from her with a mild tale of breaking the law as a teenager when I traded clothes with a scarecrow that was dressed better than I was. She was a devout lady working hard to do good in the world.

As a young lad I was taught to turn the other cheek when attacked or verbally abused but before many years I ran out of cheeks quite often.

Every time we thought we had made ends meet they kept moving the ends.

When the doctor told me at eighty-five years of age he couldn't make me any younger I told him, don't even try—just work hard to make me older!

Here We Go Again

A priest, a rabbi and a minister were fishing in a boat a hundred yards from shore and it was very hot. The priest announced, "I'm really thirsty so I'll walk over there to that park and get a drink from the fountain." He climbed out of the boat and very carefully made his way to shore hardly getting his shoes wet.

"My," said the minister. "What faith Father Ryan has!"

Seeing his chance the Rabbi answered "Yes, one has to have faith as Jesus did when he walked on the water," and with that he started for the water fountain as soon as the priest had climbed back into the boat.

The minister was on the spot after witnessing what he supposed were two miracles. After much discomfort and praying for faith he stepped over the side and sank to the bottom.

"We should have told him about those old pilings just under the surface that we always use. Now he is all wet and still thirsty, but when we get him back into the boat let's not say a word while we are still ahead."

Jackpot!

An elderly gentleman with a heart condition won the Megabucks lottery. His family was reluctant to break the news to him as they feared it might trigger a fatal heart attack so they asked the local priest to call on the lucky winner to tactfully give him the news. The good Father began by asking, "What would you do if you were to win the lottery?"

"I would give all the money to the church," was the reply.

The priest flipped over dead of heart failure.

A Vermont farmer won the lottery and was asked what he would do with the $10,000,000. "Oh, I would just keep farming until it was all gone."

A widow bought her first lottery ticket and won millions of dollars. A neighbor inquired, "What will you do first now that you have all that money?"

Without hesitating she answered, "I will pay off some of my bills."

"But what will you do about the rest?"

"Oh, they will just have to wait."

Some retired ladies in Florida had organized a bridge club and when Julia inherited $17,000,000 from her deceased fourth husband, all the other ladies were eager to hear about her newfound wealth.

"Do you still miss him?" was one of the first questions.

"I miss him terribly. Sometimes I feel as if I can't stand the remorse. I would give $5,000 if I could just get him back."

Not to let it go at that, one of the gossipy women asked the *big* question. "Did you marry him for his money?"

"But of course not!" was the reply. "However, as time went by I realized that was the only way I could get it."

How to Get Results

An old pastor down in Atlanta reached the point where he needed to be replaced and take his well-deserved retirement. The young, newly ordained priest sent to him needed considerable training as he was very hesitant and shy. While he gave his lackluster sermons in a monotone voice, people started to doze off and this was followed by an abrupt decline in contributions when the basket was passed. The old priest could see drastic changes were needed—and soon. After a good deal of meditating he took the young replacement aside and suggested he have a glass of water on the podium. "When you get stuck for something to say, take a slow drink of water. This little animation will hold the congregation's attention while you think of what you are going to say next." This remedy did not help very much and the people still dozed off or were bored no end. Meanwhile the collections continued to get smaller.

The young man felt himself a complete failure so one evening after a Knights of Columbus meeting he joined some of the members in a local bar. Someone ordered him a glass of gin that he soon disposed of and became somewhat more talkative than usual. This was followed by two or three more and the glass of gin reminded him of the glass of water he had been placing on the pulpit every Sunday morning. The next Sunday, he put a pitcher of gin and a glass right at his elbow. When he slowed down a little, he poured out a glass of gin and drank it while thinking of what to say next. After a few more drinks to bolster his courage, he really got down to business and soon the people were wide awake, shouting, "Amen, Amen, brother!" As the spirited sermon continued his listeners began to clap hands and stomp on the floor shouting, "Alleluia! Alleluia!" Some even threw their hats into the air—the collection basket overflowed.

The old priest joined his protégé on the steps of the church to share the adulation and compliments as people shook their hands. There were smiles all around. "Well, young man, you really had them in the aisles but it might be a good idea to tone it down just a bit. For instance, David merely *slew* Goliath, he didn't stomp the living —— well, let's just say, *daylights* out of him!"

Heaven Is Such a Fun Place

Fifty nuns down in San Jose, Costa Rica, were being treated to a vacation bus trip up to Liberia, over one hundred miles to the north. The volunteer driver was quite reckless and when he tried to pass a car on a hill, he lost control and the bus plunged five hundred feet down a cliff into the rocky surf. Of course there were no survivors but the high-spirited nuns were warmly welcomed to heaven by St. Peter's deputy, St. Isadore. After a few days they were asked how they liked it and was there anything that could be done to make their stay more enjoyable. "Oh! It is better than we expected, just wonderful!" they all chorused. "The only thing is," one of them confessed, "we just can't get around fast enough. We haven't found Sister Agnes or Mother Theresa yet and all the biblical characters we have always looked forward to meeting...."

"OK, OK," interrupted St. Peter who had been listening. "Isadore, take care of this right away." In a short time the girls were all fitted out with roller skates and went zipping off at great speed laughing and chirping away.

Meanwhile, overworked St. Peter finally took time off to see how Chief Bongo Bongo, a former cannibal who had been converted to the faith just before his death, was adjusting. "How are things, Chief?" inquired St. Peter.

"Well, it's really nice but I still miss the palm trees and the island life I left behind. However, I really appreciate the 'meals on wheels' program you initiated last week. I feel right at home."

He Tried

Sam Dole led a rather adventurous life and avoided any religious activity much to the dismay of his parents and acquaintances. He cheated on his income taxes, carried on unscrupulous businesses, swore often and could never be relied on to tell the truth. Upon his untimely death he arrived before St. Isadore pleading for mercy on his soul. Sam used all of his persuasive powers that had worked for him on earth but

St. Isadore merely countered with long lists of Sam's indiscretions.

"In fact," said Isadore, "you have broken every commandment over and over during your lifetime so how can you expect to enter heaven? It wouldn't be fair to all the good people who have led exemplary lives."

Now Sam slid easily into his role as negotiator. "Now I've heard of a place called Purgatory where we can make amends for our sins so you should be able to resolve this without sending me to hell."

"Hold on here!" interrupted St. Isadore. "Don't try to bargain with me and anyhow, St. Peter makes the final decision. I'm just his assistant."

Not to give up, Sam came back with, "I could arrange to make things easier for you up here, you know, if you could just slip me through on the sly without St. Pete even knowing about it. Now how about that Purgatory deal?"

"Sam, if I could be persuaded to accept any kind of deal with you it would still take more than five thousand years to get you off the hook." St. Peter's frustrated deputy responded.

Sam persisted. "Tell you what, my friend, make it four thousand years and we will have a bargain."

Isadore was already on his cell phone trying to reach his boss. When St. Peter arrived to confront the shyster he gave the verdict: "To hell forever, end of discussion."

Sam made one more pathetic plea, "OK, but couldn't you just work out something with the devil to give me some little concession, maybe a cooler place in some corner?"

As Peter walked away he said over his shoulder, "I'll make only one little concession. Isadore, furnish Sam with a handbasket."

Connoisseurs

On an island just west of Fiji, a cannibal chief, Bano, invited a neighboring chief to lunch and after a fine repast his guest graciously invited him to his island for a great feast planned for the next day. "What are we having?" asked Bano. "My son-in-law," his friend replied.

After several days Chief Bano ended his sojourn and returned home to find all of the tribe very ill. "What happened? What have you been eating?" the chief asked.

"We ate a fat man who came here."

"What was this fat man wearing?" inquired the chief.

"He had on a brown robe with a rope around his waist," someone responded.

"Alright, now tell me how you cooked him."

"We boiled him in the big kettle in water with a little noni juice," replied the chief cook, "and he was delicious."

"Why, you fools, that was a Friar, you never boil a Friar! You *fry* a Friar!"

The Moral of the Story (or How I Lost $700,000)

All too often as we go through life, we take offense at someone's spontaneous remark. Nearly everyone at some time says something inappropriate because of surprise or sudden anger, words we would never use under normal circumstances.

We read in the Bible, "Whoever says, 'You fool' is in danger of hellfire." I've always remembered this but never fully subscribed to it given my propensity for encountering genuine fools quite often. I've always hated being called a fool but few people can attest more to the need to forgive after being called a fool than I, after a near elopement incident many years ago.

Agnes Snodgrass was not considered a prize by the young men around the village where she lived but she had several pluses in her favor. Agnes was brought up by a strict mother who taught her how to cook, to sew and be a good housekeeper. She needed these advantages because she was not really pretty, not good looking at all and had a rather full figure for a young girl. It's beyond my recollection just how we became involved. It just sort of grew like some kind of mold or fungus on a crop of tomatoes.

My habits haven't changed much from those days. I still stop to pet dogs and cats and sometimes share my lunch with squirrels and rabbits. It's hard to say whether Agnes took advantage of my kindheartedness or if I may have overdone the "be kind to your neighbor" bit. Before I realized it things were out of hand and Agnes was talking more and more about "double harness," "getting hitched" and "starting out together."

Partly because I didn't always listen to what she was saying and also because her father used these phrases when talking about his horses, it didn't sink in until one evening she excitedly began talking about how romantic it would be to elope. Bang! Now that's when the 1,000-watt light bulb came on. For some reason I couldn't get another word in and her plans kept tumbling out faster and faster. She assumed silence indicated consent but she apparently never heard of enforced silence. When she stopped for breath I was speechless with fear, shock, dread, despair, apprehension and many other bad feelings.

Poor Agnes never had much dating experience but probably day-dreamed, fantasized and romanticized throughout her girlhood. (I've since learned that other girls do these things, too.) Anyhow, she either assumed or wanted me to assume that we were now engaged and what more romantic development could happen than a story-book elopement. This was not a sudden, passionate, spontaneous escapade but a very carefully thought out and deliberate plan. Agnes was well organized—no argument there.

While I was still in a bewildered state of mind, Agnes skillfully maneuvered me into a participatory role—reluctant and unwilling but a participant. She would have preferred a Rudolph Valentino approach, white horse and all, but she knew I would never put on those Arab-type robes and no way could I lean down from the saddle and sweep up one hundred and sixty-five pounds from in front of a tent. For the sake of practicality, she elected to go the more conventional ladder-up-to-the-window route. To say Agnes was practical would really be an understatement.

Somehow, when the night agreed upon—by Agnes—arrived I found myself in the Snodgrass yard and easily found the ladder hidden in a hedge of rose bushes under her window. It was heavy. I wondered how her father ever managed to put that ladder up to the hayloft until I remembered how he did everything because Mrs. Snodgrass told him to.

With some difficulty I placed the ladder and climbed up to the open bedroom window. As I slipped into the semi-darkened room it seemed unusually quiet. I expected Agnes would be up and ready to leave but it looked like she still wanted that abduction story to tell her grandchildren how she was forcibly stolen from her father's house. Well, what the heck, I thought, I'll pay the two dollars and play the game.

Next came the hard part. I expected she would put up a little token resistance but she jumped around like a wounded buffalo. This alarmed me because her thrashing around and yelling would wake up the whole household. Well, two can play this game, I thought, and being pretty rugged in those days, I muffled her with a pillow case and got a good grip on her to carry her out and down the ladder. She seemed half again as big as I recalled and even though she was still in her nightgown, she put up a realistic struggle. Why in the world wasn't she dressed for traveling? Just like Agnes to overdo the realism.

Once outside on the ladder things began to get a little hairy. The ladder began bouncing up and down and it seemed like I was carrying two one hundred pound bags of chicken feed in my arms. Then the pillow case worked loose and she began to scream and carry on until we almost fell off the ladder.

Suddenly another window opened and Agnes leaned out screaming, "Over here, over here, you damned fool! That's Mother you are carrying down!" That really made me mad when she called me a fool! Before I could answer, her mother sunk her teeth into my shoulder and the ladder started to crack, splitting from end to end. As it collapsed down the wall of the house, Mrs. Snodgrass and I landed in the hedge of rose bushes with more of her out of the nightgown than in it. There was real determination in my efforts to escape but every time I started to get out from under, Mrs. Snodgrass would scramble on top to escape the thorns of the rosebushes. Finally the yard light came on illuminating a scene from my worst nightmares, only it was real, and I ran all the way home before I realized Mrs. Snodgrass would be missing the large piece of flannel nightgown I still clutched in my hand.

Needless to say, our relationship ended that awful night. Nobody called me a fool and got away with it. But here is the moral of the story because if I had forgiven that remark I would have shared the $700,000 inheritance Agnes received a year later. Perhaps we should look at it this way: Agnes has the $700,000 and I have the scar of her mother's teeth marks in my shoulder. We each have something to remember that episode.

Think Carefully

While still in college I was invited to visit a family in Newport, Vermont, on the Canadian border. My friend introduced me to a captivating, very pretty girl I couldn't help but take a liking to. She was 110 percent French Canadian and came from a very strict family that adhered to old French customs. We rapidly developed a close relationship and finally Bernadette Marie Lajoie suggested it was time for me to ask her father for her hand in marriage. I was somewhat taken aback by the suddenness of it all and wasn't expecting in that day and age to have to ask for her hand. Why not ask for all of her if I had to go through with such a humiliating chore. Bernadette was quite adamant as this was a family tradition and a prerequisite to any plans for marriage.

After some deep thought on the matter, weighing my dread of encountering her father against my feelings for such a desirable girl, I was motivated to agree to bite the bullet. I put it off for a time but finally with great reluctance went to the house and broached the subject. Mr. Lajoie asked me a number of questions in his strong French accent and just as I thought the ordeal was about to end and in my favor he dropped the bombshell. "Are you prepared to support a family?"

"I think so," I replied.

The head of the Lajoie family leaned forward, looked me in the eye and said, "Think carefully, there are twelve of us."

I bolted out the door without a backward glance and didn't set foot in Newport again for fifty years, and even after that long interlude I kept glancing over my shoulder.

How About That!

A man was about to put a quarter into a parking meter that had the red flag for overtime when a policeman stepped up and covered the slot with his hand. "Sorry mister but this car is parked overtime and it's too late to put more money in. I'm writing a ticket and you will have to pay the five dollar fine. You can put more money in after I leave."

"Nice try," said the man, "but I wouldn't pay a nickel if you are writing the ticket. You are rude, greedy and don't deserve to wear that uniform. I think you should be reported."

The cop grew very belligerent, whipped out his book and started to write up several complaints. He announced, "I'm giving you about a dozen citations in addition to the overtime parking—insulting an officer, refusing to pay a fine and this car has a broken taillight, defective tires and worn out wiper blades. You are going to pay plenty before this is over."

As he walked away, the man said, "I'm just glad that isn't my car."

Another Mona Lisa?

For about five hundred years people have admired Leonardo De Vinci's painting "The Mona Lisa." We have wondered about and tried to guess the reason for that half smile, that not-quite smug, unrevealing expression. Something of the Oriental inscrutability, combined with that "cat that got the canary" look is there. Something inwardly satisfying never to be revealed must have taken place. That smile can arouse a sense of anticipation for some men and quite possibly more than a little envy among some women.

For somewhat less than five hundred years, I have had the unique experience of occasionally looking up to see a Mona Lisa smile, much prettier than the original but certainly just as unrevealing and mysterious. It happens every time anyone, for one reason or another mentions my possible demise. No sooner do I say something about "winding up my ball of yarn" or "putting on my wooden overcoat" than it happens. There is a pause, I look across the table and there is that "you will never really know" expression. Just as surely as the question will never be asked, the answer will never be known.

It all started less than a year after we were married. A recurrence of a fever, contracted in Trinidad during the war, had laid me so low that my chances of recovery seemed quite remote. Many thoughts passed through my mind as I lay there with all the work of the farm at a virtual standstill and so many other things left unaccomplished. I was thinking I was surely too young to die when a rather disturbing step was taken without consulting me. Two of my brothers, the hired man and a neighbor suddenly appeared and at my wife's direction picked up the bed while I was still in it and carried it through the big double doors into the north parlor. Everyone who had died in this eighteen-room house during the past forty years had first been moved into this north parlor and for me it seemed like the final preparation. Not a word was spoken but the silent message was the most ominous sound I had heard in quite a while.

Each link in the chain of events that followed seemed to lead straight towards my putting on that "wooden overcoat." The doctor summarized his daily visit with "Humm." This was the only prognosis and no one elaborated on his "Humm," leaving me in the dark (literally and figuratively since the shades had been drawn as soon as someone noticed me watching my colts frisking in their nearby pasture).

There was considerable coming and going. Six sisters-in-law and their mother were lending a hand with household chores and taking turns playing nurse. There had probably never been so many pretty girls in that house at one time before. There was continuous conversation—in French, of course—and those sparkling clean young girls who looked after me helped make the time pass more pleasantly. In fact, I began to worry less and less about the farm work and started to dwell on how long I could hold off the grim reaper.

Eventually, it seemed there was a good chance of my outfoxing the old rascal. This feeling manifested itself one day when I just couldn't help patting one of those pretty "nurses" while she straightened out the bedclothes. Those dark eyes flashed and she snapped (in English) "Watch that, brother," to which I replied, "I have, for the past fifteen minutes." She apparently submitted a whispered report on my condition since there was a lull in the conversation in the kitchen after she left my room.

There was a noticeable change in the atmosphere after that little interlude. Chores were handled a bit more briskly and efficiently. The doctor did not come the next day but someone else did and I was quite sobered by the visit. The doctor must have decided he could be of no further help—I had always heard you feel better and look a little better just before you go. Why else would they call Father Leonard? Just as I was beginning to almost enjoy my (temporary, I hoped) helpless state, it was very grave indeed to learn everyone else knew something about my condition that I didn't.

Obviously, the good Father had been summoned to hear my last confession so I started a hasty examination of conscience. I recalled his annoying habit of repeating out loud whatever he heard. This presented a problem with half my in-laws listening at the door and the other half waiting at home for details. My last chance for salvation was beginning to look like an open forum.

I elected to start out with one of my minor transgressions, recalling that I had once exchanged clothes with a scarecrow that was dressed better than I was. "Stole some clothes did ye?" he fairly shouted. I pretended to suffer a slight relapse which left me too weak to continue. "Come, come, young man, you're not the only one on his death bed today!" The relapse became a mild shock, but Father lessoned my feelings somewhat with several comforting remarks, to the effect that a young, pretty widow unencumbered with children would not have to grieve alone for very long. This relieved my mind considerably and the dear old soul left quite satisfied I'm sure.

An hour later I heard a loud "pinch," which was the sound my important papers drawer emitted when opened. Through the partly opened door I saw a hand removing what appeared to be my will and insurance papers. Another loud "pinch" and the drawer was closed.

By late afternoon, a most delicious aroma floated into the north parlor from the kitchen, a good forty feet away. Corned beef and cabbage—my favorite dish—prepared with loving care for my last meal. How thoughtful of my bride to remember what I enjoyed most for supper. Because of my feeble voice and the uninterrupted conversation out in the dining room, there was no way to get my thoughtful wife's attention until they stopped at suppertime to say grace. "Dear," I called. "Please bring me some of that corned beef and cabbage so I can have one last good meal before I go."

"Not on your life," she answered, "We are saving that for the wake."

The next morning, while I was on the tractor mowing alfalfa, I tried to figure out the meaning behind that Mona Lisa smile I had seen at the breakfast table. Would she have really saved the corned beef and cabbage had I not made such a speedy recovery? Had she taken my condition as lightly as she appeared to? Or was it possible she had accomplished a masterpiece of strategy to snatch me from an untimely end?

It is as impossible to read the meaning of that smile as it is to put the questions into words. One thing is for sure. Every time I see that Mona Lisa smile we are sure to have corned beef and cabbage for supper.

Garage Sale

Any farmer worth his salt avoids throwing away anything that might be of use in the future. It requires self-discipline, stoicism, determination and the ability to preserve these valuable items casually without attracting the attention of family members, especially the *one*. Truly, now, one of the great joys of practicing this art is to store the treasure hoard without any particular system. Pieces of harness mixed with old tractor parts, broken wrenches, chain links, old baler and chopper parts add some charm and nostalgia. This method enables one to enjoy the coolness of the garage on a hot day or escape the winter wind for a longer interval, one of the privileges allocated to the "boss" or the "Major" as he was called on our farms.

Another important benefit that comes from searching at random through the whole collection is rediscovering some forgotten object you will surely need in years to come. It's good to know it's there and a written inventory is not only tedious and boring but downright impersonal. With such strong feelings about this delicate subject, it came with some emotion to have an ultimatum leveled at me on what would otherwise have been a pleasant day. My formidable chief-of-staff entered the "HIS" part of the storage area (she terms it disaster area) and declared firmly and irrevocably that all that junk must go immediately to the landfill. In other words, to the "dump" as I still refer to it. I associate only useless clutter of no value whatsoever with the word "dump."

Compliments on her pert appearance and the special beauty that comes to the maturing woman had no effect on her decision. I pretended she was trying to humor me, that it was just a big joke being played on me, but this ploy backfired with a threat that one of us might be sleeping in the office. None of the normally successful reasonings prevailed so the realization struck me that I was about to lose many cherished possessions as well as a philosophy that seemed a right and privilege justly earned.

Returning from the last load to the "dump," I cherished the memory of my collection that ran back over seventy years. It had all started with the collection that came with my first farm that I bought from Floyd Keese, an avid collector who had tools and remnants of tools going back to the 1850s. I was somewhat apprehensive when I found my chief-of-staff carefully labeling boxes filled with leftover items from the "HERS" side of the storage area. I didn't expect she would share in my sacrifice with total commitment and she certainly didn't appreciate how much being separated from what had become my old friends would affect me emotionally. She never knew the attachment I had for such things as my Dad's old kerosene lantern (that leaked), the snaffle bit we kept when I sold old Peggy, the nose rings from all the bulls I had ever owned, a carburetor from Pat Harte's old F-30 tractor, the elevator chain from a 1913 Buckeye threshing machine and the thousand other objects laid before the bulldozer's blade.

Carried away somewhat by her display of participation on her (small) part, I was about to suggest it wasn't necessary to strive for total discard when I noticed a list of articles on a clipboard. Now why would anyone care to keep a record of things to go to the dump? When I married this girl I realized she came with many fine qualities. Her mother assured me she was a very nice girl and inclined to frugality and efficiency to a high degree. She displayed her flair for full utilization of time and material during the war as she knitted gloves for unknown servicemen while she attended school at a convent in Canada. It occurred to her that should a recipient of these gloves lose an arm, as occasionally happens in combat, the other glove would be useless to him. Because of this concern for labor lost, she devised a most ingenious little pleat in the thumb of each glove to enable one to wear it on either hand. If you were to examine a glove knitted for soldiers today by a Canadian nun you would find it carries this same feature.

It was not until I attempted to load one of the boxes onto the truck that the revelation came to me that items from the "HERS" side of the storage were destined for a GARAGE SALE. Now garage sales have always seemed to me to be a kind of redistribution of storage problems, a revolving neighborhood clutter syndrome. I immediately felt a lessening of guilt for having trucked a good part of my collection to the "other farm." Many farmers have what they call the "other farm" that can cover a multitude (of things). A place to plant a new crop you are skeptical of, a place to experiment and now, for me, a place to stash part of my useful junk. My thoughts and feelings were somewhat tempered due to these timely and provident actions I had taken in not committing all of my possessions to the bulldozer.

Since my part of the dispersal was completed, I attempted to learn why the "HERS" items were valuable while my useful collection was labeled junk. I hardly raised an eyebrow at the boxes containing every baby food jar we had acquired in starting five boys but boxes labeled "row ends" aroused my curiosity. These "row ends" turned out to be seeds left over from seed packages we had bought for over twenty-five years of gardening. The seed companies could very well package in smaller amounts or I should have lengthened the rows in the garden. I never realized over all these years there were so many seeds left over and certainly didn't guess they had been saved.

The next items were boxes the old Addison County Trust bank used to mail out check books. These were neatly labeled "Short pieces of string" and underneath typed in small print,

"Too short to be used." I thought that these trivial items should go to the dump surreptitiously but surprisingly these items sold well at the garage sale.

Fortunately I withheld my indignation over the unfair allocation of value to the contents of the two storage areas. I was also better prepared the day after the garage sale to show compassion as she wept inconsolably after receiving a letter from her sister Rena in Chicago. Rena advised her of a practical use for the short pieces of string. "Put them out for the birds to use for building their nests." Frugal Madeleine cried for a week.

Sedgwick and Fifi

The late Doctor Bertram Towers of Herefordshire once owned what was perhaps the most intelligent bird in history. His parrot, Sedgwick, was capable of playing a winning game of chess, could discuss philosophy, politics, history and many other subjects. Mathematics posed no problem for Sedgwick while his extensive vocabulary enabled him to carry on conversations with quite intelligent people.

Realizing the parrot's abilities would most likely be transmitted to offspring, Dr. Towers spent several years searching for a suitable mate for Sedgwick. Intensive investigation in several countries turned up not a single female parrot compatible with Sedgwick and certainly not of comparable intellect. Time was running out for Dr. Towers to start a progeny of super intelligent birds and the problem weighed heavily on his mind as he realized Sedgwick was getting on in years as well.

One of his colleagues heard a rumor that a widow only a few miles from the doctor's home possessed a female parrot of the same species as Sedgwick, was exceptionally intelligent but, of course, lacked the superb training and study the doctor had been able to provide his bird. Nonetheless, the good man hurried over to the widow's estate and explained his plans for starting a line of super parrots but was unprepared for the scolding he received from Lady Gladstone. She would under no circumstances subject her poor Fifi to such a humiliating ordeal. How gross of the doctor for even suggesting such a degrading proposal. This was a crushing blow to Dr. Towers and more than a little disappointing to Sedgwick who, of course, was privy to the negotiations. In his preparations for a new approach to the widow, Dr. Towers learned of a serious problem developing for the owner of Gladstone Manor. It seemed that long overdue taxes on the estate were due for collection and she had very little, if any, of the 2,500 pounds required by the collector.

Armed with this critical information, the doctor hurried over and paid a second and very gracious call on Lady Gladstone. He again tried to impress upon her the value of his proposition to science and the urgency of the matter due to Sedgwick's age. Very tactfully, he mentioned he would be willing to reimburse her as much as 2,500 pounds but avoided any reference to the upcoming collection of taxes. Even so, the mere mention of that figure rang a bell in the woman's mind as the tax problem had been in her thoughts a great deal of late. "Perhaps, my dear sir, solely in the interest of science, we might arrange something but this terrible sacrifice on Fifi's part should be noted and go down in the annals of scientific records. Never will so little a one give so much for so many. Absolute privacy must be maintained and I shall see that the heavy drapes in the parlor are drawn until this scientific venture is accomplished."

With this pronouncement, the doctor hurriedly wrote out a check and rushed out to the car to get the overjoyed Sedgwick. The doctor was practically overcome with emotion because at long last it seemed the most cherished dream of his career was about to be fulfilled. His elation was exceeded only by Sedgwick's.

Lady Gladstone carried out her preparations even to providing soft music and a subdued lighting effect. During the proceedings, the only audible sounds outside the lovers' parlor were the occasional dignified sobs of Fifi's mistress and the nervous pacing and mumbling of Sedgwick's master. When it seemed, by mutual agreement, that the objective must have been accomplished, the door to the room was opened. The scene caused the poor widow to scream in horror while the doctor was at first surprised and bewildered but soon slightly amused. The room was filled with feathers from floor to ceiling. Sedgwick was pulling the last feather from poor Fifi and shouting over and over, "For 2,500 pounds I want you nude, by Jove, NUDE!"

Heathcliff and Margo

The phone rang at 2:45 a.m. "Heathcliff, heah," was the sleepy answer.

"Heathcliff, this is Margo."

"Oh, I say, I don't recall anyone named Margo."

"Well you must remember me, Heathcliff. I'm that redhead you took about last autumn and introduced as such a marvelous sport to everyone, an extraordinary good sport. Then we had that smashing affair at the lovely seaside inn in Sidmouth."

"Oh, yes, yes, Margo, it's quite possible I should remember you but why are you calling me at this hour?"

"Well it seems, Heathcliff, that I'm pregnant and you are responsible."

"Oh, my word! What a revolting development!"

"And furthermore, Heathcliff, either you must marry me or I shall commit suicide."

After a rather long pause, Heathcliff answered, "Gads, Margo, you really *are* a sport awern't you!"

Birds and Bees

"Bernard, I think it's about time you spoke to Ronald about the birds and the bees!" announced Mrs. Carlisle.

"Oh, my word! I don't quite know how to broach the subject to the boy," replied her husband.

"Bernard, go right up to his room this minute. He's getting on, you know, so take care of this right now."

"Yes, Dear, of course. I suppose you are right." Bernard knocked on his son's door and said, "Ronald, your mother and I have been talking and decided you and I should have a talk about the birds and the bees."

"Come in, come in, Father."

"I'll get right to the point, my boy. Do you recall that trip to Paris you and I took last summer and that little interlude with those showgirls?"

Ronald smiled and answered, "Yes indeed, Father, I do."

"Well, Ronald my boy, the birds and the bees do somewhat the same thing. Good night, son."

Alien

As Cedric relaxed in his garden reading the *London Times*, a small space ship whirred down onto the lawn beside him. Hardly glancing at his visitor and certainly not losing his line on an article he was perusing, Cedric saw out of the corner of his eye a strange, very small creature with antennas protruding from his forehead and a most repulsive countenance. The little green and yellow visitor climbed down from his glowing craft, saluted smartly and said in an electronic voice, "Take me to your leader." Without a second glance, Cedric answered, "Nonsense, old chap. What you need is a plastic surgeon."

A Bleak Outlook

Basil and Bertram were on a hunting safari in Africa. Suddenly, their guides and bearers turned back and ran for a jungle thicket, leaving the two hunters in a rather wide clearing with only a single tree in the middle. They soon saw why their party had abandoned them when a pair of gigantic lions came bounding towards them. In their haste to get to the lone tree for a refuge the panic stricken men dropped their rifles but managed to scamper up the tree just inches ahead of those long sharp claws. "We will wait them out," said Basil. The lions took turns guarding what they perceived as a great feast while their quarries suffered thirst for two days and nights, during which time the two men ate every leaf on the tree. Finally, on the third day Bertram remarked with typical British reserve, "Somehow I don't like the look of things, Basil."

Reconsider

A ninety-three-year-old member of the Gentlemen's Club was voted the winner of the Outstanding Achievement Award for the year because he had married a twenty-six-year-old woman. The next year he was again honored because he reported he was the father of a new son. After the applause died down a member stood up and requested to relate an incident that took place on a hunting expedition.

"A ninety-year-old man accompanied us into the bush and the first morning he picked up his walking cane instead of his gun. Before long a lion charged us and the old fellow raised his cane and shouted, 'Bang, bang.' Miraculously, two shots rang out and the lion dropped dead. Now tell me what do you think of that?"

An eighty-year-old member gave his opinion: "I would say somebody, probably a much younger man, pumped a couple of rounds into that lion."

"My point exactly," replied the storyteller.

Good Memory

An elephant lumbered down to the water hole where many animals gathered to refresh themselves and enjoy each other's company. Giraffes, hippos, and other large creatures splashed about the shallow pool while the elephant playfully squirted them with his trunk. Suddenly, the elephant stopped abruptly and stared across the pool. A large turtle was resting on a flat rock. The elephant splashed over to the turtle and upon reaching it quickly kicked it hard sending it hundreds of feet over the treetops to crash into the jungle with fatal results.

"What in the world was that all about?" asked the giraffe.

"Fifty years ago that turtle bit me on the end of my trunk. It's still sensitive and you can see the scar right here," replied the pachyderm.

The other animals crowded around and one ventured to ask, "After *fifty years*? What kind of memory do you call that?"

The elephant ambled off and said over his shoulder, "You *could* call it Turtle Recall."

After the Campaign

A politician ran an aggressive and very expensive campaign. He spent all the money from donations as well as his own savings but failed miserably to win the election. Being desperate for any kind of work (he had never worked a day in his life) and being turned down everywhere he finally applied for the job of sheepherder on a ranch. He was told there were two other applicants ahead of him so he decided to wait as he was determined to take any work, any place, any time. The next day the first applicant went off up the mountain with the sheep at daylight but came down alone in the late forenoon saying it was too quiet and lonely up there.

The next would-be shepherd took the sheep up early the next morning singing cheerfully, quite sure he would get the job. He returned about mid-forenoon complaining that the sheep smelled awful and took off down the road.

Now the once politician took his turn, confident he could handle whatever challenges came his way. He also left early in the morning with the sheep. By nine o'clock the sheep came back down.

Irish Stories

The gifted and skilled Irish storyteller Hal Roach was certainly the most extraordinary comedian of his time. He regaled his listeners with tales of the Irish people without demeaning them. He used their proclivity for overcoming adversity and sad times by keeping a sense of humor and fortifying themselves with Irish whisky and Guinness. Hal was able to enliven his stories about his countrymen in a way that made everyone, including the subjects of his jokes, laugh till the tears came. He gave one stellar performance in Dublin about thirty years ago with the best stories I've ever heard although a few were an Irish version of tales I had been telling for many years. After some of the best of them he would say, "Write it down! It's a good one!" He laughed at his own jokes.

Here are a few of his best that he had told me to write down.

Tough!

Murphy told everyone his wife drives him to drink.
"Lucky guy," said Quinn, "I have to *walk* down to the pub."
"My wife stays up until after two o'clock in the morning," said O'Riley.
"Why?" someone asked.
"She waits up 'till I come home."

"Hurry! My wife is having a baby!" a man shouted into the phone after dialing 911.
"Is this her first baby?" the operator asked.
"No! No! It's me, her first husband!"

The Fountain

The city of Limerick decided to build a fountain and delegated the clerk to handle the business such as hiring the contractor and was even entrusted to work out the terms of the contract. Advertisements were placed in newspapers and out of the several responses the clerk selected three contenders to come in for interviews. Murphy from Dublin, Riley from County Clare and Casey from County Cork.

Murphy from Dublin was called in first. "How much for the fountain?" asked the clerk.
"3,000 pounds," came the reply.
"Break that down for me."
"1,000 for the material, 1,000 for the labor and 1,000 for me."
"Wait outside," said the clerk.
Next came Riley. "How much for the fountain?"

"6,000 pounds," stated the man.

"Break that down for me."

"2,000 pounds for the material, 2,000 for the workmen and 2,000 for me."

"Wait outside."

So now the wily, foxy Casey from County Cork presented himself all smiles and confident.

"How much for the fountain?" asked the clerk.

"9,000 pounds," said Casey.

"Break that down for me."

Casey put his feet on the desk and tilted back in his chair, hands behind his head, completely relaxed. "3,000 pounds for you, 3,000 pounds for me and we can give the contract to Murphy, the man from Dublin!"

Molly

Molly was strolling one evening with her husband when she saw a women's clothing store with beautiful gowns displayed in the window. "Wouldn't I look lovely in something long and flowing?" So her husband threw her into the river.

Hal loved children and reveled in stories about them.

Holy Family

The good sister was teaching her class about the holy family. "Children, I want each of you to draw a picture of the holy family's flight into Egypt." Little Mary presented hers first—a drawing of an airplane with three people in the back and one up front.

"Explain your picture, Mary, and tell us who the people are in the plane, start with the three in the back."

"Well, there is Joseph and Mary and the little baby Jesus."
"And who is in front?" queried the teacher.
"Why that's Pontius, the pilot," replied Mary.

"Who are the Eskimos?" the teacher asked the class.
One little boy raised his hand and answered, "They are God's frozen people."
Hal didn't spare those who had a thirst for drink.

Doolin

Doolin was addicted to drink. He woke up one morning with a terrible thirst and no money. He walked down and stood outside Kennedy's pub waiting for it to open and wondering how he could manage a few drinks without any money. About then, a hearse went by, hit a bump in the road that caused the rear door to fly open and the corpse to slide out into the street. The driver, busy driving the horses was not aware of what happened so continued on. Doolin looked up and down the street—no one in sight. Quickly he ran out and lifted the well-dressed body to a standing position and with an arm around his shoulders waltzed him into the pub. He propped his newfound friend up with his elbows on the bar and keeping a good grip on his bar mate ordered two whiskeys. Doolin downed the first two and ordered two more. Later when he told Hennessey, the bartender, to bring two more drinks he was told he already owed two pounds and could he pay for it all.

"Oh, my friend here will pay, see how well dressed he is, new suit and tie but he needs one more to perk up a little."

Two more drinks came sliding down the bar and when they were disposed of, Doolin went to the men's room. Hennessey, somewhat alarmed to see Doolin gone, stood in front of the corpse and said, "You owe me three pounds and I want it now!"

Getting no response he took the man by the shoulders and shook him hard. Of course the corpse fell to the floor just as Doolin came back in. Seeing Hennessey leaning over the body he shouted, "What have you done to him? Dear God! He's dead! You've killed my best friend!"

"I had to," replied Hennessey. "He pulled a knife on me!"

Confessions Irish Style

Sean O'Neal slipped into the confessional surreptitiously. After some hesitancy he began, "Father, it's a terrible thing I have done. I blew up seven miles of British Railway!"

"Well, my son, I will give you absolution but for your penance do the stations." (The good Father probably didn't mean the Stations of the Cross)

Cassidy

Cassidy came home at three in the morning and was making a lot of noise on the stairway.

"What's all the noise?" asked his wife.
"I'm trying to get a keg of Guinness up the stair," said Cassidy.
"Leave it and bring it up in the morning."
"I can't," replied her husband, "I drank it."

Kids Say the Darndest Things

Danny was a good kid but very slow in school and sometimes he didn't respond well to criticism. After one exasperating episode the teacher decided to send a note home to the boy's father. At the close of the message she had written, "Your son is positively illiterate!"

His father immediately picked up the phone and called the teacher stating Danny was not illiterate because, "His mother and I were married several weeks before he was born."

You Can't Always Win

During one period while raising our five sons I attempted to correct their grammar all too often. They occasionally made fun of me by uttering phrases intended to get my attention or at least provoke me. For example, when I asked ten-year-old Thomas what kind of day he had, his response was, "Me and Pierre had funner'n hell."

Some time later, a neighbor took our three youngest boys to a movie.

Next morning Michael related, "Last night we saw a fox coming home from the movie!"

"Now Michael, what makes you think a fox would have gone to a movie?"
"Let me rephrase that," Michael answered.

A few words have always annoyed me. "Got," I felt, should seldom be used. I have even corrected people suggesting they say, "I have to go" rather than "I've got to go." All too common we hear something like this: "I've got to go to Burlinton, Vermotte, to get a hunnert and twenny dollars from my account."

At a PTA meeting one evening a teacher gave a short talk and my neighbor Percy Mack recorded over forty "You know, likes" in just a very few minutes. My own jargon has equally as many or more shortcomings but it still makes me wince to hear, "You know, like."

In spite of my blundering and annoying (to them) teaching, all of our sons became more articulate than their father.

Home Schooled?

Sister Claire was teaching a class on the Bible. "Michael, who knocked down the walls of Jericho?"

"I didn't do it," answered her student.

Somewhat taken aback at the obvious neglect of his homework assignment, the good Sister resolved to speak to his parents. She encountered his mother on the street and told her about her son's remark. "If my son said he didn't do it, —-!"

Startled somewhat by the woman's irate manner, Sister Claire decided she should confront the delinquent boy's father in an effort to get his parents more involved with Michael's progress. Gaining entrance to the boy's home, she found Michael's father relaxing and thinking about getting a job—a difficult chore because the man would not work during a week that had a Friday in it. He thought manual labor was the Spanish ambassador.

"Today I asked your son who knocked down the walls of Jericho and he answered that he didn't do it. Needless to say I was shocked at his response."

Michael's father interrupted. "Now look here, Sister, I don't want any trouble. How much did that wall cost?"

Just a Thought

A man was leaving the courthouse after a severe chewing out by the judge when he turned and asked the judge, "What would you do if I called you a SOB?"

"I would fine you $500 and send you to jail for five days," responded the judge.

"Well, what if I were just *thinking* you were an SOB?"

"No problem," said the judge, "I can't charge you for what you are thinking."

"In that case, your honor, I *think* you are an SOB"

Wow!

Bruno was, to say the least, not at all bright. Acquaintances just shook their heads at Bruno's blundering through life. He returned home one day to find his wife in the arms of a man who had a bad reputation in the community. Bruno strode over to the desk and drew a large pistol out of a drawer, loaded it and placed the muzzle to his own temple.

His wife panicked and started to scream. "Oh! Bruno, don't do that. I love you and will make this up to you, please, please don't do this!"

"You shut up!" shouted Bruno. "You're next!"

He Did It His Way

At class reunions, people try to figure out how this one or that one succeeded or failed. Oscar had been voted the least likely to succeed by his classmates but at his twenty-fifth reunion he was the only multimillionaire. Naturally everyone wanted to know his secret so in answer to their queries, he responded, "Well it's simple. I operate on a three percent profit, buy something for a dollar and sell it for three dollars. I sell things for ten cents apiece or two for a quarter. It always worked for me."

One girl I did marry had a boyfriend in the Navy. She cried for days when he had to go overseas—to Staten Island.

The other girl I didn't marry went to the movies with me one evening. When we arrived at my car after the show we found it locked up tight with the keys still inside. While wondering how to solve the problem, Betty helped by suggesting, "It's such a nice night we can ride home in the rumble seat."

In a Hurry

Frank Murray was a hustler. He rushed from one thing to another with his mind on what he needed to do next. One morning he was planning his day's work on the farm, things he would do as soon as he delivered his milk to the dairy. In those days farmers put their milk into ten-gallon cans and kept them cool in a tank filled with water before taking them to the "milk plant" every morning. Frank proudly drove his new International pickup truck down past the store, waving at people along the way and pulled up to the unloading ramp to wait his turn to unload his milk. He nodded to the other farmers and made sure they had time to admire his new truck. He was quite chagrinned as he reached for a can of milk. There were no cans of milk. He had forgotten them and it was plain to the other men what had happened so they had a good laugh. Thinking about his day's work and anxious to show off his new truck he had driven away empty and had to make an embarrassing second trip.

The Riddle

Amos Dimmock returned from a trip after midnight and found no one at the Burlington Airport to meet him to provide a ride home. Fortunately, there was a van for that purpose and after the driver waited a few minutes and no one else showed up for a ride, he and Amos started off on the fifteen-mile ride to the Dimmock homestead. After a silence (Amos was tired) the driver said he had a riddle and proceeded to ask Amos to figure it out. "It's not my sister and it's not my brother but we have the same father and mother, who is it?"

"I don't know," Amos answered sleepily.
"Why it's me!" replied the driver.
"That's a good one," drawled Amos.

Later on, during an evening at the American Legion in Vergennes, the talk had slowed down and Amos was called on for a story or joke. Without the several drinks he had consumed, Amos would never have come up with the stupid conundrum but he launched into it and asked if anyone knew the answer. "Who is it?" he asked and of course everyone said, "It's you!"

"No, it's not me! It's that van driver up at the Burlington Airport!"

Slow Learner

Because I was such a poor student they kept me in the second grade over and over until it became an embarrassment—not only for me but for the teacher and the school board. There was only one solution—move the kid *up*. One morning I woke up excited because I was finally going into the third grade. I was so excited I cut myself shaving. I was the only kid in the third grade with a driver's license.

Trying To Play Hooky

One beautiful spring day my folks left early to go to the city on business. Thinking of how nice it would be to spend the day out in the woods instead of the boring classroom an idea came to me. Picking up the phone, I rang the school. When they answered, I changed my voice to as deep a pitch I could achieve and announced, "Francis Angier can't go to school today, he's terribly sick."

"Oh, that's too bad. Who is this speaking please?"
"This is my father talking."

Really Old

There was a teacher who taught in a small country one-room school. She was very old and when someone got up nerve enough to ask her age, she replied, "When I was in school they didn't teach history. That's how old I am."

A Teacher Remembered

In the fourth grade we students were required to give a factual report once a week. It had to be newsworthy or at least interesting for the class. Because of my intense interest in aviation from the time I was able to read, all books and magazines having to do with flying provided me with information about many events most people paid little attention to. In 1932, the year I was in the fourth grade, it was commonly believed that Charles Lindbergh was the first person to fly an airplane across the ocean. Actually, he was the first man to fly nonstop from New York City to Paris, France. He flew alone for thirty-three and a half hours in a single engine plane, a remarkable accomplishment, but others had crossed the ocean by air beginning in 1919. Still, because of the publicity and notoriety Lindbergh had earned by his historical feat in 1927, it was generally assumed for several years that he was the first to fly the Atlantic.

My report began with an account of Alcock and Brown, two British pilots who flew a World War I bomber from Newfoundland to Ireland in 1919—about the same time the U.S. Navy was attempting to fly to Europe with three flying boats supported by warships stationed along their route every fifty miles or so. One aircraft finally made it to Portugal. Shortly after these flights the British flew a dirigible (lighter than aircraft) with nearly thirty people on board from England to Canada and back, so about seventy people had crossed the ocean by air before Lindbergh.

The teacher, a cross, terribly strict and often rude woman, interrupted me in the middle of my talk. "Francis Angier! Why are you telling us all this nonsense? Everyone knows Charles Lindbergh was the first to fly across the ocean. Sit down right now and don't you ever try anything like this again!" She was one of those people who had a very narrow interest in events and probably didn't read very much. She should not have been a teacher.

I never tried to prove my historical report to her. I could have brought her numerous accounts of aviation history but just tolerated her for the rest of the school year. Years later I realized she may have been under great stress. Family problems, health issues, a disappointing love affair or a dismal upbringing may have caused her to act irrationally. Still, actions like whacking a student across the knuckles with a heavy ruler or administering harsh lickings with a paddle made her very unpopular with all her students.

Overheard

"My wife and I were happy together for twenty years but then we got married."
"Dan, are you spitting into the flower vase again?"
"No, but I'm getting closer to it."
Two Irish women were at the laundry when one of them remarked, "Ye never loved your husband did ye?"
"No, I never loved me husband," was the reply.
"Then why is it you had twelve children by him?"
"I was trying to lose him in the crowd."

"Daddy, why did you and Mom get married?" his teen-aged son asked.

"Did you ever notice that white shotgun hanging over the door?" his father replied.

"Horace, how did you decide to marry me?"

"Well, your dad wanted me to marry your older sister as a start to get his seven girls out of the house. We were leaning on the barnyard fence looking over his little pigs when he suggested he might throw in one of those pigs to boot if I would take Ethel off his hands."

His wife queried, "So, knowing you, how could you turn down an offer like that?"

"I said I wouldn't take Ethel but would take you if he would throw in two pigs and by golly, we had a deal!"

Everyone has a favorite weather prediction—

"It will be a long dry spell if it doesn't rain."

"Red sky in the morning, sailor take warning. Red sky at night, sailor's delight." But the most accurate would be, sunset in the morning everyone take warning!"

"How much did you pay for them mules you got there, Benny?"

"Didn't cost me a darn cent, Caleb!"

"Oh, stole 'em did ye?"

"No, they was strays and followed me home."

Caleb allowed he had also recently bought a nice team.

"How much did you pay for your team, Caleb?"

"Well, Benny, not as much as I expected to but more than I ever thought I would."

These are two Vermont methods to avoid revealing the cost of their personal transactions.

"If I had $4,000 to get married I guess I would buy a used car. It's easier to back out of a garage."

"How did your rake get busted, Charlie?"
"My hired man drove it up onto a rock."
"Is that the same hired man that had to marry your daughter?"
"Ayah," replied the neighbor.
"Gads, that man is a clumsy one!"

Tim and his wife were having an argument and were giving each other the silent treatment. He didn't want to be the first to give in but he suddenly realized he had to get up at 5 a.m. the next morning for an early business flight. To not break the silence (and LOSE) he wrote a note, "Please wake me at 5 a.m." and left it where she would find it. When he woke up next morning it was 9 a.m. and he had missed his flight. He noticed a note by his bed. It said, "It's 5 a.m. Wake up."

A man said to his wife one day, "I don't know how you can be so stupid and so beautiful at the same time."

His wife responded, "Allow me to explain. God made me beautiful so you would be attracted to me; God made me stupid so I would be attracted to you."

A couple drove down a country road for several miles, not saying a word because an earlier discussion had led to an argument. As they passed by a barnyard filled with mules, goats and pigs the husband asked sarcastically, "Relatives of yours?"
"Yup," his wife replied. "In-laws."

Billy Bob and Lester were talking when Billy told Lester, "Ya know, I reckon I'll take a vacation again this year but I'm not relying on you for suggestions as to where to go. Three years ago you said to go to Hawaii and Marie got pregnant. Then two years ago you said Bahamas and Marie got pregnant again. Last year you sent me to Tahiti and darned if Marie didn't get pregnant!"

So Lester said "What are you going to do different this year?"

Billy Bob says, "I'm taking Marie with me this time."

Why is a government worker like a shotgun with a broken firing pin?

Because it won't work and you can't fire it.

My mind works like lightning. One brilliant flash and it is gone.

Well Prepared

A lady was being questioned about her four marriages. "Tell us about all those marriages and why are you now married to a mortician?" one of her new friends at the retirement home asked. "Well, in my twenties I married a stockbroker and when he passed on I was in my thirties and I married a comedian who gave stage performances but he ran off with a showgirl."

Another curious woman asked, "What did your third husband do?"

"Oh, he was a minister and spent a lot of time talking to me about the scriptures but he was a bit older and died when he was eighty-eight years old but I was only in my mid-seventies and, being lonely, I married a nice man with a great personality."

Now the circle of women drew their chairs up closer and they could hardly wait to learn why she would feel comfortable living with a funeral director.

"Oh, he completes the story of all four marriages. Number one was for the money, number two for the show, number three to get ready and four to go!"

Ritual

An elderly Vermont lady retired to Florida and never changed her lifestyle. On one of my visits with her on a Wednesday afternoon I concluded the conversation by stating, "I guess I'll go home and take a shower." Remembering her Saturday night baths she remarked, "My goodness, where has the week gone?"

A Good Deed

An older couple was struggling to make a living on a small farm during the early days of the Depression. By raising most of their food in well-tended gardens, milking a few cows, and raising pigs and chickens while being very frugal, they were comfortable because they did not hanker for things they could get along without.

One morning after chores, a man came to the door and said he was hungry but was willing to split wood before being fed as he had noticed a neat pile of wood near the shed. The couple convinced him he should eat first and fed him a substantial breakfast while they listened to his story about his losses. The bank had taken over his house, he sold his car to buy groceries and the business he worked for had shut down, and now he was traveling about looking for work. He worked a good part of the forenoon on the wood so his benefactors insisted he stay for lunch.

While he worked, the Christian couple had talked it over and decided to give him the man's old suit. "You seldom wear it and we don't go anywhere very often so he may as well have it as his clothes are pretty well worn," said the wife. Her husband agreed and when the man left, he reluctantly accepted the gift and carried it away neatly folded in a large paper bag. A while later the wife confessed she had put the 100-dollar bill given to her on their twenty-fifth anniversary in the pocket of the suit. Her husband was nearly overcome by her generosity but he knew she was the kind of woman who would share anything she had even with a stranger.

That evening the destitute man sold the suit for $3 without ever taking it out of the bag.

Gone With the Wind

Nanny and Billy were grazing on a steep slope just below a movie studio in Hollywood. Typical of goats, they licked the glue off from tin cans and nibbled pieces of paper as well as other curious items. Billy was trying to be really macho by leaping over stumps and climbing steep rocks while Nanny goaded him on to more daring exhibitions. They encountered a huge pile of discarded film—a worn-out copy of the hours-long epoch *Gone With the Wind*.

Nanny challenged Billy to see how much of the celluloid he could devour. Before long Billy's stomach was distended but he realized he could not stop taking in the film because it was all in one very long strip. He had no choice but to eat the whole pile. As he stood gasping and burping with his stomach distended, Nanny mischievously asked "How did you like the film, Billy?"

"Frankly, my dear, I liked the book much better."

Always on Tuesday

The date was fast approaching for graduation from Aviation Cadet to officer with gold bars and silver wings, a really momentous occasion after eight months of rigorous training. I decided to take my dress shoes into nearby Seymour, Indiana, for some minor repairs at a small shoemaker's shop I had seen on one of my infrequent trips into town.

After leaving the shoes, all my time was taken up with paperwork and preparing for the great day. I bccame so engrossed in my chores the shoes were forgotten until I had returned from my leave and been posted to Chanute Field, Illinois. They were written off as a wartime loss.

Some thirty-five years later as I was going through my trunk full of mementos I found the receipt for those shoes and wondered if the little shoemaker was still in business and what he had done with my shoes. As we were planning to attend my 457th Bomb Group reunion in Minneapolis the next year, as well as visiting some of the air bases where I'd been stationed, I put that receipt in the glove compartment of our car.

Freeman Field, near Seymour, Indiana, was our first stop so we drove around the base and then looked for the old shoe shop in town. Amazingly we saw the sign and entered the place. A bald, shuffling old man came to the counter and stared at the wrinkled piece of paper I handed him. Looking over his glasses at me he asked, "Are you the one who brought these shoes in here?"

"Yes, I did. My name is right under the date—September 21, 1943."

He turned and shuffled into the back room mumbling, "You wanted heels and soles, right?"

"Probably, I can't remember that far back."

We could hear him rummaging around for some time. My wife remarked that he must be senile or didn't realize just how far back 1943 was. Finally he returned and handed me the receipt saying, "They will be ready Tuesday."

That's the Kind of Man He Is

Our son John was a stockbroker for a firm that was purchased by a multimillionaire. When the new owner came to visit his new acquisition, John was selected to escort him from the airport and introduce him to the staff and other brokers gathered in a large auditorium. As they walked down the sidewalk towards the headquarters, John caught his shoe on a metal grating and peeled the sole back so it just flopped up and down. Deciding it would be too embarrassing to stand on the stage to introduce the very wealthy man with his shoe in disrepair, John apologetically said he would have to stop at a store for a minute to buy a pair of shoes. It was then he discovered just what kind of man he was with. Putting his hand on John's arm the wealthy man said, "Let me take care of this." John protested but the man insisted. Reaching into his pocket he drew out a huge roll of large bills and peeled off the rubber band. He then knelt down and put the rubber band around John's shoe securing the sole. And that's the kind of man he is.

Lawyer and the Duck

A big city lawyer went duck hunting in rural Vermont. He shot a duck but it fell into a farmer's field on the other side of a fence. As the lawyer climbed over the fence, an elderly farmer drove up on his tractor and asked him what he was doing. The lawyer answered arrogantly, "I shot that duck and it fell into this field and now I'm going to retrieve it."

The old farmer responded, "This is my property and you are not coming over here."

The indignant litigator said, "I'm one of the best trial lawyers in the country and if you don't let me get my duck I'll sue you for everything you own."

The old farmer smiled and said, "Apparently you don't know how we settle disputes out here in the country. We settle small disagreements like this with the 'three kick rule'."

The lawyer asked, "What is the 'three kick rule'?"

The farmer explained, "Because the dispute occurred on my land, I kick you the first three times, then you kick me three times and so on back and forth until one of us gives up."

The attorney thought about the unique contest and decided he could easily take the old man. After all, how hard could he kick, so he agreed to abide by the rules. The old codger slowly climbed down from the tractor and walked up to the attorney. His first kick planted the toe of his heavy work boot into the lawyer's groin dropping him to his knees. His second kick to the midriff brought up the lawyer's last meal. With the lawyer on all fours, the third kick sent him face first into a fresh cow pie.

Summoning all his strength, the lawyer managed to get to his feet, wiped his face with the sleeve of his jacket and said, "Okay, old man, now it's my turn so get yourself down from that tractor!"

The old farmer smiled and drawled, "Naw, I give up. You can have the duck."

Sorry

A man with weak vision tried to cross the street and was hit by a car. The driver didn't stop to help the man but sped away and the next car struck the poor man and he didn't stop either. In all, five hit and run drivers ran over the body. They all thought the victim was a lawyer but the last car to arrive at the scene stopped because he *was* a lawyer.

There have been similar cases when motorists thought they had hit a politician and just drove on. I looked up the word "politics" in the dictionary and found it is a combination of two words: "poli" which means many and "tics" which means bloodsuckers.

An inexpensive way to learn your family's history is to run for public office.

The Give-Away

A sixteen-year-old finally had his driver's license and managed to borrow the family car for a night out but was admonished to come home early. The lad slept quite late the next morning but as he came into the kitchen his father inquired, "Did you get home late last night?"

"No, it was early," the boy answered honestly.

"You must mean early in the morning, Son, or else I will have to talk to the paper boy and tell him not to put my paper under the front tire of the car."

A policeman stopped a girl for not wearing her seatbelt, She denied it by saying she unbuckled her belt when he approached her car so she could reach her driver's license. "Sorry, young lady, but you can't sell that story. You shut your door on the belt and I saw it dangling outside of the car. A few other things I noticed: You were talking on your cell phone, drinking something from that cup and what is that hairbrush doing on your lap?" Young girls are quite dexterous.

The wife lagged behind her husband as they walked along the sidewalk. When she was a few steps behind him she stepped on one of those scales that give your weight and fortune on a little card. "Oh look, Tom, this says I'm very intelligent, beautiful, frugal and sexy." Looking over her shoulder the husband remarked, "That's what it says but it has your weight wrong as well."

One man who was very careful of his new car ensured his wife would be extremely cautious when she used his prized possession. "You know, dear, if you have an accident your age will appear in the newspaper."

They call it a family tree because someone will always find some sap in it.

Whenever my wife and I get separated in the supermarket or mall I just walk up to a pretty woman and ask her if we can talk for a few minutes. My wife shows up in less than a minute.

A friend of mine bought and read a book, *Fifty Ways to Lose Your Lover*. He tried them all even to insisting his wife drive their car to Florida while he drove their motor home but she stuck to him like a burdock on a horse's tail. He was about to give up when they visited a huge super mall called the Galleria or something like that. It was gigantic but he lost her in five minutes.

A man wanted to get out of serving on jury duty so when he was questioned, he responded by saying, "I am very prejudiced against the man. He looks like a crook, he looks dishonest, his eyes are shifty, he dresses like a mafia member and I believe he is guilty as can be. I shouldn't be on this jury." The judge spoke up. "Take your seat in the jury box. We need a good judge of character like you. That man you described is his lawyer."

The Retired Ram

It was my pleasure to help out a Mr. Myran Boswell, an old shepherd who had a soft heart for all animals and when it came time to retire he just hated to see his flock sold to strangers. His old ram, GF (his registered name was Golden Fleece), had made him a considerable amount of money over a number of years not only by the lambs he sired on the home farm but his progeny was spread across the country. His breeding fees had generated a small fortune for the elderly farmer.

There was no way he could part with his aging ram that had lost his sight and could no longer roam the pastures. Mr. Boswell had a rather elaborate shelter built down near a spring that provided running water and had all the comforts old GF could desire. A large window on the south side let in warm sunshine in winter while the overhead storage held the most fragrant hay available, as well as clean straw for bedding. When I was called on to care for the ram the old man explained exactly what needed doing. I was somewhat baffled to see an old phonograph on a shelf in the shed until Mr. Boswell explained that the instrument was to be cranked up each day and the single record played for the blind old ram. He explained it was the ram's favorite song sung by Bing Crosby or some other popular singer and was entitled, "I'll Never See Another You." Of course GF thought "you" was "ewe" and dreamed of the old days while it played.

Dear Uncle John Letters

Dear Uncle John

Amos and I have been dating for a few years and he hasn't spent more than twenty dollars on me all this time. He forgets his wallet or leaves the table for the bathroom when the waiter brings the check. He plans our dates around free affairs or something we are invited to. What is your take on this guy?

Almost Broke

Dear Broke,

Give Amos his twenty dollars back.

Uncle John,

In my workplace there are about thirty men and fifteen women. This may sound good for me but there is a problem. Every birthday, wedding or other event to celebrate we are expected to have a dinner and present a gift for whoever is honored. The men never bring anything so we girls end up preparing a dish or a cake very often—whenever someone thinks up an excuse for a party. I really don't have the time or money to continue with these frequent affairs. What should I do?

Worn Out in Albany

Dear Worn Out,

Join the crowd. Have frequent birthdays, get married, have a baby, be the guest of honor every few weeks. If this doesn't work start bringing bad covered dishes. Your co-workers will back off a little.

Uncle John

Uncle John,

My best friend, "Joan," is single and a virgin and she wants to keep it that way. However, she confides in me that she often has "urges" and wonders if she is missing out on life. Since I am in the same state as Joan I am trying to help her through this difficult period. I've tried to help by getting her involved in church and community affairs, joining a health club, taking up a sport, traveling or starting a new hobby. Can you think of anything else I should tell her?

Single too

Dear Single,

You forgot the cold shower.

Uncle John

Dear Uncle John,

My wife clams up on me when ever we have a little tiff or if she gets a little offended. Sometimes she doesn't speak to me for days. This is very frustrating and it gets lonesome after a while. What can I do to cure her?

Shut out by "Shut Up"

Dear Shut Out,

No cure that I know of so get out during these interludes. Go down to the Legion, go bowling or relax someplace. Just be glad she isn't a chatterbox and talks your ear off.

Uncle John

Dear Uncle John,

My wife decided to go back to college to get her degree so she has been out of our house most of the time for almost two years now. She and several other college women have gone to Paris to study French history and my wife keeps delaying her departure until at present she has been in France fourteen months. I'm getting pretty lonely and really sick of my corn flake–hotdog diet. What can I do to get her to come back?

Lonely and hungry

Dear Lonely,

Wake up, Pal. Join a cooking class, get involved in social clubs, take up poker. You should have at least learned how to make an omelet by now because she ain't coming back.

Uncle John

Dear Uncle John,

I don't know how to deal with this problem. When I hang my laundry out on the clothesline my handsome neighbor always seems to come out to take his sunbath and I am getting to the point where I take a longer time out in the yard on wash day. My husband hasn't noticed anything yet but I am very tempted to go over to the fence and talk to my tanned idol. What can I do about this before—-well, before anything happens?

Tempted.

Dear Tempted,

Get a clothes dryer *now*! If you can't afford a dryer, have your husband move the clothesline to the other side of the house.

Uncle John

Inefficient Farmers

There was a shifty real estate agent back in the 1940s who often duped people into buying property that he unfairly represented. For example, "Bub" might be showing a farm to a prospect and while driving through a gap in the fence would remark, "Now isn't this a beautiful meadow?" The newcomer would stare at the large, level piece of farmland and agree to the extent this helped him make his decision to buy the farm he was being shown. Of course, the meadow on the other side of the fence was not part of the property for sale.

These deceptive practices often resulted in legal actions but the wily agent usually went free because he was careful not to actually lie to his clients as in the above example. Just a clever suggestion or remark usually resulted in a sale.

He took one out-of-state would-be farmer up into Ripton, Vermont, to show a small farm in the winter. The new owner couldn't wait for spring to arrive so he could start farming. When the deep snow finally melted he was horrified to see hundreds of boulders scattered all over the only level field on the little farm. He encountered Bub and began a tirade telling him what a terrible dishonest crook he was and he should have his license taken away.

When Bub was able to get a word in, he tried to explain to the very angry man how lucky he was to own such a valuable piece of property. "Now, sir, calm yourself, those stones extend your season up here by warming the soil sooner in the spring and holding the heat longer in the fall. Meanwhile, they break down into fertilizer—slowly of course, but all this very rich soil is derived from decaying rocks."

"Just hold on a minute," responded the angry man, "If that is true, why do all the other farmers have their rocks piled up neatly in those stone walls around each field?"

"Well, my good man, those are the inefficient farmers. They've never got around to spreading theirs yet!"

Innovative but Shifty

An old duffer moved to Largo, Florida, to retire but soon felt the need to make a little more money. He bought a small parcel of land and established a pet veterinary service and a pet cemetery as well. He offered free care for ill or injured small animals so it was not surprising that his new venture brought in many clients. However, in the very small print of the contract there was a clause stating that if the pet died while at the clinic the owners were obligated to have it buried in the pet cemetery. Very soon the mortality rate at the clinic skyrocketed. The cost of the lot was $2,700 and preparation of the remains for burial came to $1,300. All the patrons complained and some threatened to sue but nineteen spaces were filled and paid for before people started to use their magnifying glass before signing the contract.

Well?

I was building a barn in my early days of farming and finally scraped together enough money to buy the needed lumber to finish the structure. It was a cold day and the old truck had no heater so on arrival at Fred Johnson's lumberyard I ducked into the little shack that served as an office. It had a cheery wood stove for workers to warm up the chilled parts of their anatomy. I told two rugged men they could load my truck with all the 2x8 planks it would hold and off they went while I warmed up by the stove.

In a few minutes one of the men stuck his head in the door and asked, "How *long* do you want those planks, Francis?"

"Well, quite a while. I'm building a barn."

Pansy and Violet

One of the interesting families I was exposed to during my flying days in Arkansas lived up in the foothills of the Ozark Mountains. One of our planes made a forced landing up there and had to be dismantled in order to be transported back to the airfield. As part of the party to retrieve the wrecked plane, I had the experience of meeting the Venom sisters from Rattlesnake Ridge. Pansy and Violet were very curious, quite pretty but not well groomed and had a disgusting habit of chewing tobacco. While the work progressed (we three cadets were there only to observe) the captain in charge of the mechanics told us we were invited to lunch at the Venoms and we had better be there to keep on good terms with the family as the downed plane had plowed through their tobacco field and turnip patch. The Venoms were very poor, very proud but hospitable and would have been insulted had we not accepted their offer.

The grandmother had been sent to the spring near where the work was going on to fetch two pails of water. We thought we would help her by carrying the water up the hill to the house. The old lady must have been nearly as old as God, didn't have a tooth in her head but managed to keep a good grip on her corn-cob pipe. I glanced into the spring, nice clear water but home to a number of frogs. The lunch was cornmeal mush and turnips flavored with sorghum syrup. The house and its contents were not very tidy but we tolerated it all under the watchful eye of the captain.

The pilot of the damaged plane had told us there was a very nice swimming hole in the river within walking distance so my roommate and I had brought our swimming trunks along. With the family's permission we started out and the girls' mother told us Violet could join us but Pansy couldn't go swimming because her bathing suit had a hole in the knee! My roommate and I flew back to base that evening with a new and different perspective of life in America.

Say Again?

A widow with two sons in their early teens came to me for advice. The boys were getting out of hand and had begun to use foul and very offensive language so because she knew we had five sons she wondered how to deal with the problem. After listening and asking enough questions I gave my opinion. "You need to correct this problem right now before the boys get old enough to be physically dangerous with you. Go down to the karate school and get in a few weeks training before you try to discipline them again."

She decided to take my advice and the next day she began a rigorous exercise program and was soon ready to start a karate course. When she felt prepared, she set a day to teach the boys a lesson. As the older son came down stairs she politely asked, "Well, son number one, what would you like for breakfast?" He answered with a loud voice, "I'll take some of those g-d——d, #@*>^, blankety blank cornflakes by %$@#!" Before he knew what hit him he was yanked off the bottom step, spun through the air and slammed against the wall. His brother observed the violent encounter from the stairway with his mouth wide open and visibly in shock. His mother put her hands on her hips and asked, "And what would you like for breakfast, number two son?" Number two stared at his brother sliding down the wall, shaking his head and answered, "You can bet your big broad bottom I'm not going to ask for any of those #@*+ corn flakes by %$@#!"

Old Age?

The city of St. Petersburg, Florida, used to maintain several green benches along the main street where the elderly folks could sit to enjoy the sun, visit and watch the passing scene. One day I happened to overhear four quite elderly appearing gentlemen discussing how they had lived so long. One declared to the others how he had never touched a drop of alcohol and he was ninety-two years old. The second man said he was eighty-nine and attributed it to never having smoked, while the next old chap declared he had lived ninety years "so far." After some prodding by the first two as to his secret he answered, "Well, I've lived a very continent life—I left the women alone. I never chased the girls."

The fourth man had not contributed any advice as he sat on the end of the bench with his shaky hand on his cane. He was very thin and appeared to be extremely weak but finally spoke up after the other three had encouraged him to relate how he had spent his life. "I started smoking when I was ten and I've drunk about a fifth of liquor every day since I was twelve. It was about that age when I discovered girls and never lost interest in them until a few years ago." The others thought that was remarkable and pressed him to give his age. After some mumbling, twisting his cane around and showing considerable hesitancy he responded, "I'll be twenty-eight years old next week."

Snow?

One winter we were enjoying the warm sun in Florida when a Vermonter stopped by our motor home and asked, "Now tell me honestly, don't you miss the snow up there?" "Yes I do miss the snow and I go to considerable expense to miss it."

A lady in the same RV park saw my POW tag on our motor home and a purple heart tag on our tow car. Studying the POW tag she finally said, "Oh, post office worker!"

Another serious remark by a lady from Georgia was humorous in a way but not very complimentary to me. "Did you fly in World War I?" she queried. "Yes," I replied. "I stole my Daddy's draft card."

To make up for that question three ladies accosted me as I walked alone one morning on the Municipal Pier at St. Petersburg. They were all in their mid-eighties, I guessed, very well dressed, made up and apparently widows looking for men. They started a conversation with me inquiring where I was from, what I had worked at and other questions I began to think were rather personal. As I squeezed by them to make my escape, one of them leaned very close and said, "I'd like to watch you shave every morning." Perhaps I should have been flattered but never before had anyone thirty-five years past my age been so bold and no woman before or since has frightened me quite like those three professional widows. Of course, they may have just decided to be mischievous and have a little fun with me. Anyhow, they were good examples of how elderly people can enjoy life by getting out in the sun all winter instead of sitting by the stove or trying to negotiate the ice and snow while tolerating the wind and cold in Vermont.

Not Soon Enough

We were standing on the pier at St. Petersburg watching the pelicans being fed when one bird took off, apparently satisfied with his meal of fish. He needed to lighten his load but unfortunately the load splashed onto the bald head of an elderly man standing next to us. My wife told him to hold still a minute. "I'll go into the building and get some toilet paper." "Shucks," said the old fellow, "by the time she gets back that pelican will be half way across Tampa bay."

Poor Advice

A patron was having his hair cut at his local barber shop and casually mentioned he was going to Rome to visit the Pope.

"Good luck," said the barber. "You may wait for days or weeks to see him because he's too busy for ordinary folks and, by the way, what airline are you traveling on?"

"Air Italia," responded the man.

"You have made a poor choice. That is one of the worst airlines," warned the barber.

When the traveler returned everyone wanted to know how his trip went and if he really saw the Pope. "Had a great flight over and back on Air Italia and not only saw the Pope but he shook my hand and talked to me."

"What did he say to you?" asked the barber.

"He asked me who gave me such a bad haircut."

Joe Savage

Joe Savage was a "name dropper." If anyone happened to mention a celebrity Joe would speak up and declare he knew the person well and relate some personal encounter. Several men in a related business of Joe's were to attend a conference in Italy so Joe went along. Someone mentioned one of the Supreme Court Justices and true to form Joe said, "Yes I know him. We play golf together." When the name of a prominent movie star came up the other men were getting a little annoyed because Joe claimed he had dated the actress several times. As the plane circled over Rome, Joe looked down and remarked, "Well, there is the Vatican. I wonder how my old friend Pope John Paul is doing."

"Don't tell us you know the Pope!"

"Oh yes, he and I have skied up in the Alps and corresponded for years," Joe said casually.

The other men went into a huddle and decided to call Joe's bluff. "Let's get him into a taxi and go right to St. Peters Square," they decided.

When they arrived at the Vatican, Joe told them to keep watch of a certain balcony and he would bring John Paul out to wave to them. After some time Joe appeared with someone with a staff and mitered headgear.

"He's paid that person to come out there with him," one of the men muttered. One of them approached an Italian woman. "Madame, could you tell us if that is Pope John Paul with that man up on the balcony?"

The woman shaded her eyes and squinted before answering, "I dona know for sure if thatsa John Paul but that other guy, thatsa Joe Savage!"

The Letter

Just after I was liberated from a Nazi prisoner of war camp in 1945, a victim of a nearby concentration camp motioned me over to the fence. The army medics had said he was too weak to be moved and he was not much more than a skeleton. No one knew his nationality nor could they find anyone who understood his language, a most tragic wreck of a human being. He appeared to be near death but pushed a crumpled piece of paper through the wires and indicated by signs the letter was for me to take out of the country for him. It must have been very important and from the plaintive look on his face he must have been hoping I would get the message to the outside world.

At every opportunity I attempted to find someone who could translate the letter but everyone said it was written in a very rare dialect, probably from a remote area in the Balkans. After several years a language professor from a well-known university said he could not translate it but recognized a few clues as to the origins of the writing. After some time he contacted me and said he could direct me to an individual, Dr. Unger, who should be able to help.

Professor Unger had been a brilliant man but was now just a human derelict, mentally deficient, an alcoholic and given to bizarre behavior. He reluctantly agreed to meet me in the middle of a high railroad bridge over the Mississippi River at Vicksburg. He appeared at the agreed upon hour in the middle of the structure dressed in rags and clutching a whisky bottle. There would be a fee he announced in a heavy accent—one hundred dollars. Considering his condition it seemed like an unwise investment but he assured me if he could not decipher the letter he would give me the money back.

The poor creature clutched the letter in one hand and the hundred dollar bill in the other. The half empty whisky bottle was cradled under his arm. He slowly began to read. Suddenly as he read a few lines to himself his eyes opened wide, he stared at me and began to shake uncontrollably muttering, "This is clairvoyance, impossible, how could you have kept such a message on your person for so long, what in the world was that man thinking of?"

I tried to tell him to read it to me. I was beside myself to know what was on that piece of paper I had carried for years. "I don't believe you will want to hear this. It is catastrophic!" said Unger. "But I will do as you ask."

Just then, the bottle slipped out from under his arm and he made a desperate effort to secure it but lost his balance and tumbled over the railing of that high bridge. Down into the muddy Mississippi a hundred feet below the man fell with a mournful wail. The letter and my hundred dollar bill fluttered slowly down out of sight. So I never found out the contents of that strange letter.

Taking Turns

Dan was spending some time in the hospital but seemed to be recovering as indicated by his behavior one morning when the nurse came in to attend him. "Good morning," she said cheerfully. "Such a nice day! Are we ready for our bath?"

"We are always ready for our bath, aren't we?" responded Dan as he sat up with a big smile.

The nurse began to wash his face, neck, shoulders and chest. At that point she handed him the washcloth and said brightly, "Now it's your turn."

Dan started to wash her face and neck but her attitude changed abruptly and she was no doubt the cause of his being released from the hospital that very afternoon.

In the Fast Lane

Several people were in the doctor's waiting room when a nun burst in. She was hiccupping nonstop and gasping for breath. Everyone was very concerned so one lady spoke to the nurse and suggested the nun should go in immediately to see the doctor and to everyone's relief she was taken from the waiting room ahead of all the other patients. In only a minute or two the nun came rushing out with no signs of hiccups but screaming as she dashed out of the office. The doctor just stood in the door smiling much to the consternation of the other patients who couldn't wait to learn the cause of the bazaar incident. "How did you cure her hiccups so quickly and why was she so upset?" someone asked.

"I just told her she was pregnant," the doctor explained.

Thanks a Lot!

Tony's wife was really angry because he forgot her birthday so she decided to give him an ultimatum. "Tomorrow morning I want to look out and see something in the driveway that will go from 0 to 160 in no time flat!"

Tony followed her demands to the letter. When she looked out in the morning she saw a package in front of the garage door. She took it into the house to open and found a new bathroom scale. It went from 0 to 160 instantly.

Funeral arrangements are being handled by the local cremation services.

Note: One way to always remember your wife's birthday is to forget it once!

New Fur Coat

An acquaintance of mine came into a bit of money and his wife went on a shopping spree in, of all places, Paris! When she returned, the couple invited quite a number of friends to their recently remodeled home. Clara was showing off her purchases to the houseful of guests who were quite impressed. After a time Clara went into her bedroom and came out dressed in her finest but everyone was awed by her stunning fur coat. As she glided about the room posing like a model she brushed by me allowing the soft fur to touch my face and arm. She paused slightly, no doubt to get a compliment so I felt a handful of the material and giving her a smile remarked, "Woodchuck, isn't it?" There was a very loud silence followed by a bright flash of lightening emanating from Clara's green eyes. She didn't say a word to me at the time nor has she ever spoken a word to me since.

Bachelorhood

Before my separation from active duty after World War II, I purchased a large farm— large for those times anyway—and took over the farm the day after my release from duty. Next war I will take a whole year off before starting work. For a bachelor, the eighteen-room house (the hired man and his family occupied a six-room apartment) was pretty big. The women folk who worked at the places where I had to do business talked as if they felt sorry for me and made suggestions ranging from finding a wife to managing my household chores. They all belonged to the local Grange, an old farm organization struggling to survive in a changing world. Those nice ladies were adamant about my joining the Grange and practically dragged me to a meeting of the group. It was just not my thing and that was the last meeting I ever went to. Not to let the issue drop, the dear ladies got together and bought me a large *Bachelor's Cookbook*. When I finally found time to look at it I threw it into the trash can. Sometime later one of the Grange members asked me if I used the cookbook. "Of course not!" I answered. "Every darned recipe started out the same way. The first words were, 'Take a CLEAN dish!' What bachelor in his right mind would be able to do that?"

Looney Lucy

On one of my first post war active duty assignments my wife invited her two younger sisters along for the adventure of traveling to Texas and the possibility of meeting young men. Of course, we had our three young sons with us as well so there was a subtle reason for including two helpers to manage the children and help care for the large house we rented. The girls had no problem finding work and because they were attractive soon began dating. Things went along fine until Lucy brought a young man to the house for approval or disapproval. Peyton was quite obnoxious, wiser than everyone else, snobbish and inclined to say the wrong thing all too often. None of us were favorably impressed.

The girls went on a double date to see a movie that turned out to be hilarious. Lucy didn't go just to spend more time with Peyton but because she really wanted to see the show. The other young man in the foursome was an airman from North Carolina, very polite and considerate and somewhat apologetic for Peyton's rude manners. When the show ended Lucy couldn't stop laughing. In fact, she laughed all the way to the house in spite of Peyton's insulting remarks about her state of mind. He went so far as to refer to her as "Looney Lucy."

When he arrived at our place a few nights later the girls had been picked up by co-workers from their office to attend a party. Peyton began to question me about Lucy's mental history and had she ever acted as foolishly as she did after the movie. "Aren't you concerned about her condition? Is she here? I'd like to talk to her."

"No, she's not here. They came after her this afternoon," I answered honestly.

"Oh, the poor girl!" Peyton lamented. "I hope it doesn't turn out to be very serious or *permanent.* Throckmortan has a good mental department. I just knew she needed help.   That *is* the mental hospital isn't it? I'm going down there right now and do what I can to help her through this!"

Before I could straighten things out for him he dashed out the door and took off in the rain for Throckmortan about seventy miles to the southwest. He called about midnight from the hospital. "Lieutenant, that was a dirty rotten trick to send me off down here. I spent three hours trying to see her until they finally told me to leave. She never did come here and you knew it. You have seen the last of me but you haven't *heard* the last of me!"

And indeed we didn't hear the last of Peyton because we laughed about the episode many times over the next fifty years. I felt sorry he made the long drive in the rain but if he hadn't been such a smart aleck we could have stopped him. At least I didn't lie to him because someone did come after Lucy.

Not So Crazy

There used to be an insane asylum up in Waterbury, Vermont. A smart executive-type had a tire go flat right next to the fence that kept the residents of the hospital from wandering off. The driver decided to change the tire himself so he could tell people how mechanically inclined he was. After jacking up the car he removed the studs holding the wheel on to the vehicle, being careful to place them in the wheel cover. As he stepped back his shoe knocked the receptacle over and the five studs fell down through the grating of a storm sewer. The business man scratched his head and said aloud, "Now what will I do?"

An inmate out for his walk had been watching the procedure through the fence and spoke up. "Why don't you take a stud off from each of the other three wheels to hold your spare on then you can drive it a few miles to a garage?"

"A brilliant idea!" said the surprised driver. "Tell me, my good man what is a person like you doing in this place?"

"Well, I may be crazy but I'm not stupid!" was the reply.

Another inmate of the same institution was visited by a former neighbor who asked, "How do you like it here, Henry?"

"I can tell you one thing, Earl, it sure beats farming," Henry answered.

"Who told you that you know anything about farming because I know you worked in the city all your life."

"God told me all about farming," was the response.

At that point the man in the next bed jumped up and shouted, "I did not!"

In A Hurry

I dashed into a supermarket up in St. Albans to get a dozen eggs and started through the express checkout lane. The clerk pointed up at a sign over the cash register, "NO MORE THAN TEN ITEMS." She counted twelve eggs and would not let me through so I had to get into a long queue in the regular checkout. I was in a hurry and by that time a little frustrated so I mentioned my encounter with the woman in the express lane to the clerk at the checkout counter.

The pleasant lady accepting my money told me that the other clerk used to work for the Vermont Motor Vehicle Department. "Those bureaucrats wanted you to always dot your i's and cross your t's when you filled out your applications. One little discrepancy and you were sent back through the line. She still has that same mentality."

His Version

Pete was a real "Town Character." He was certainly unique. He listened intently to every bit of conversation then hurried off to be the first to spread the news. Pete's method of travel was to run as fast as he could with his body stretched out horizontally and his heels flying up higher than any other part of him. He was never seen walking and no one could run close behind him because of those high-flying heels.

One morning he visited the blacksmith shop to hear the latest gossip or stories. One older farmer who only talked in horse and wagon terms had a riddle that baffled his listeners.

"Why is a tree across the road like a dead dog's tail?" he queried. No one could guess the answer so with a satisfied chuckle he gave the solution: "Because it stops a waggin!"

Pete bolted out the door and ran with his longest strides to the store to try out this hilarious conundrum on the old-timers gathered about the pot bellied stove smoking cigars and chewing tobacco. "Why is a tree across the road like a dead dog's tail?" asked Pete breathlessly. Although most of the group still drove a horse and wagon in those days they couldn't give Pete an answer. Pete was then in his glory as he blurted out, "Because it stops a *buggy!*"

Money Isn't Everything

Three brothers were mourning the passing of their father who had been a very successful business man. The mortician told them they could have the final viewing privately before he closed the casket which had an automatic lock when closed and could not be opened again. This was something the old man had insisted on in his instructions for his funeral as he was a very private man. He insisted on finality to the end as he always did in business transactions.

One of the brothers was quite emotional. He addressed the other two: "Dad loved money so much I'm going to put five thousand dollars into the casket. He would like that." After he had placed the money near his late father's right hand the second brother showed his respect by putting another five thousand dollars near the deceased's left hand. Brother number three was very much like his father and loved money more than almost anything else. He fidgeted a while then scribbled out a check for fifteen thousand dollars, threw it into the casket, scooped up the ten thousand dollars cash and slammed the lid shut.

A tight-fisted old farmer from Addison, Vermont, died and was greeted in heaven by St. Isadore, one of St. Peter's deputies who interrogated the candidate at length on his qualifications to enter the gates. "Tell me, what did you do for charity in your long life?" asked the deputy.

Drawing himself up proudly the frugal old farmer answered, "Well, I gave fifteen dollars to the Bishop's Fund in 1947." Isadore furrowed his brow and decided to confer with his overworked superior, St. Peter. "This old farmer from Addison, Vermont, seems to have only one meager qualification. He says he gave fifteen dollars to the Bishop's Fund in 1947." St. Peter reached into his robe and took out fifteen dollars. "Give him his money back and tell him he can go."

One other frugal—let's go ahead and say *stingy*—individual not only loved money but told his wife on his deathbed he wanted to take some of it with him. "Just put a few dollars into the casket," he pleaded. "I'm sorry, my dear husband, but I've already checked into it and the U.S. mint says they aren't allowed to print money on asbestos."

Poor Choice

Dugan married late in life and may have been drunk when he was wed to the ugliest woman in Ireland. To complicate his life even more they were married by a justice of the peace rather than in the Catholic church. This act alone might alienate Dugan from his ninety-year-old father. After several months Dugan got up the courage to visit his father and present his wife.

The old man was in shock. Straight away he pulled Dugan into a hallway and gave vent to his disgust. "What in the world were you thinking of? Where did you find such a creature?

She's bow legged, pigeon-toed, cross-eyed, bald as a billiard ball and has a figure like a stunted oak tree. She's ———."

"Father, Father, there's no need to whisper, she's deaf as well."

Note: This is similar to a story Hal Roach used to tell before some women's organizations complained. He told me to "Write it down."

Skinny-Dipping

An elderly farmer in Louisiana owned a farm and built a large pond near the back of the property. Seeing it was suitable for swimming he fixed it up with picnic tables, fireplaces, horseshoe courts and planted some apple and peach trees.

One evening he decided to go down to the pond as he hadn't been there for a while and took a bucket along to bring back some peaches. As he neared the pond he heard voices shouting and laughing. As he arrived at the pond he saw a group of young women skinny-dipping in his pond. When they saw him they all went to the deep end of the pool. One of the girls shouted, "We are not coming out until you leave!"

The old fellow frowned and said, "I didn't come here to watch you ladies swim naked. I'm just here to feed the alligator."

Justifiable Retribution

An incredibly inventive engineer developed a technology to cause statues to become animated. He knew of a monument to a Confederate general mounted on a beautiful horse so at the first opportunity he attached his machine to the horse's ankle and turned on the generator. The general stirred, climbed down from the horse and drew his sword from its scabbard. The amazed engineer asked, "General, what is the first thing you want to do after being immobilized for one hundred and thirty-five years?"

"Son," replied the Civil War hero, "I'm going to kill me a million pigeons!"

Downhill

Eric, a retired stockbroker, was appalled by the tremendous waste he observed in dumpsters behind major stores. Huge amounts of bedding, vacuum cleaners, tools, furniture and valuable items in perfect condition and never used were destined for the landfill. Most had just been returned by customers who decided they didn't want the item or had discovered some very minor flaw. Unfortunately, many of the discarded pieces had been rendered useless by slashing or cutting off vital parts. However, Eric, a frugal Vermonter, after viewing the waste on his morning walks decided he could select unused and undamaged items from the dumpsters to sell or give away as well as making small repairs to some.

He began to visit the huge piles of goods to pick out the most valuable to take home before the landfill trucks came. It became his hobby and many families saved substantial amounts of money while Eric was pleased to have a part in reducing the accumulation of trash. One morning as he was in a dumpster searching through the contents and tossing out anything he felt was worth saving, a man who used to work with Eric in a stockbrokerage office came by on his morning constitutional. He stopped in amazement when he saw Eric emerge from the container. "Eric? Eric!" he said. Then taking in the scene he shook his head sadly and pressed a $5 bill into Eric's hand. As he walked away he was mumbling "Poor man, Poor man."

Smart Choice

A ruthless king was offended by actions and remarks one of his knights had made. "For your treachery I have decided to have you executed," announced the king.

"But Sire, I have been a loyal subject and soldier but my observations have led me to the conclusion that changes must be made in the training of our new recruits. My intent is to improve the morale and strive for more efficiency while applying more humane treatment," the young knight stated.

"You have usurped my determination to maintain strict discipline and unwavering loyalty to me. You are hereby condemned to death as an example to the other knights," replied the King.

The knight pleaded for mercy and the other knights expressed their support for him until the King made a concession. It was agreed in a signed order and witnessed by an assembly of loyal citizens that the condemned man could choose his method of death. "What is your choice?" demanded the king. "I choose to die of old age," was the answer.

The Siege

Siegfried and Ludwig had squabbled over the family fiefdom, Brundhofen, for years. Their father had left the castle to Siegfried because he had shown the most interest in the family history and seemed to be the best choice as the archivist to carry on the Brundhofen lineage. As a consolation Ludwig was assisted in seizing a grand castle with extensive holdings in Bavaria but he was never satisfied because he had desired to be the owner and master of Brundhofen. Both brothers maintained large military forces, Siegfried to defend his holdings and Ludwig with the goal of eventually driving Siegfried from the ancestral home.

Siegfried had decided the only solution was to attack his brother's stronghold and leave it in such a weakened condition as to no longer be a threat. He wanted to achieve peace although he realized that could only come after considerable bloodshed. He felt he could accomplish this by reducing Ludwig's army and destroying their ability to attack Brundhofen.

Meanwhile, Ludwig had been training his men and building siege weapons until he felt strong enough to begin his conquest. Ludwig would destroy Brundhofen if necessary to drive his brother out. He conscripted all the peasants in his villages, assigning the men to support the army with the wagon trains of supplies and the women to prepare and cook meals for the entire force.

The battering rams, catapults and other engines of war were checked and rechecked, the archers and assault teams were briefed. The march required three days along a circuitous route to prevent alarming the countryside and the entire attacking force rested out of sight of the castle in defilade the night before the assault. This was to ensure the men would be well rested from the march. Everything was in readiness for a do or die attempt and scouts reported it would appear to be a complete surprise.

Early in the morning the siege machines were hauled into position while the army was positioned on three sides of the castle. The hillsides were covered with men and horses but no activity had been observed from the battlements of Brundhofen castle.

Finally, Ludwig rode up to challenge the defenders but all was still quiet. One lone peasant was leaning over the parapet with a large mop over his shoulder. "Where is everyone?" boomed Ludwig. "I've come to take the castle and no quarter will be given until Siegfried surrenders unconditionally. You, there, where are the defenders?"

The peasant shifted his mop to the other shoulder and answered, "They've all gone over to your place."

Worked Every Time

When I was young I had *one* bumper sticker. It read, "This car stops for all blondes and brunettes and will back up five hundred feet for a redhead."

The Cabbage Patch

Cadet Chuck Atkins had an engine failure flying over Arkansas and being a really calm, quick-witted young pilot he casually banked around and glided safely into a field. He was near a long field of cabbages and he saw the only house around was at the far end of the field so he picked up his parachute and walked towards the house.

He was passing a dilapidated outhouse when a woman came out of it rearranging her dress. She was quite startled to see a stranger in his flying suit and carrying the parachute on his shoulder as she had not heard his plane as it glided down silently. Always the gentleman, Chuck took off his helmet, bowed gallantly to the lady and remarked, "Mrs. Wiggs, I presume?"

For you youngsters, "Mrs. Wiggs of the Cabbage Patch" was a popular third-grade story of a woman who lived alone in a field of cabbages. Chuck remembered the story, as I have, although it had been eleven years since he had read it. So what other appropriate remark could he have made? After all, the story could have been true and Chuck may have thought he was meeting the *real* Mrs. Wiggs!

Fanny

Fanny was the town gossip and self-appointed monitor of the local church's morals. She always stuck her nose into other people's business and although most of the community disproved of her activities, they feared her sharp tongue enough to maintain their silence. She made a mistake, however, when she accused George, a new church member, of being an alcoholic when she observed his old pickup truck parked in front of the local bar one afternoon. She told George and several others that was evidence enough of the kind of person he was.

George, a man of few words, stared at her for a moment then just turned and walked away without defending or denying anything. Later that evening, George quietly parked his old truck in front of Fanny's house, walked home and left his truck there all night.

Sam's Club

Greg had been badgering St. Isadore for months to get a pass to go back down to the world to visit his friend Sam Klam without much success. Isadore had emphasized how he couldn't approve of such an unusual request anyhow because it was up to his boss, St. Peter, the keeper of the keys to heaven, and he was too busy to be bothered with frivolities.

Finally Greg thought of a new tactic. His main reason to visit Sam would be to convince him to change his ways and prepare for salvation because Greg thought heaven was a real fun place. St. Isadore considered this idea of saving another soul but reminded Greg that his own entry was allowed with great trepidation and he would really be on thin ice if he were to break the rules while on "spring break" so to speak. After some lengthy consultations with his superior, Isadore reluctantly told Greg he could go down to see Sam but he must take his harp, carry it around with him at all times and must absolutely bring it back up when he returned.

Greg lost no time in making it down to Sam's place of business, a rather sleazy disco, noisy and smoke filled. The two old friends spent a rollicking evening and slept it off the next morning until Greg received a call from Isadore ordering him to return to heaven immediately. Greg had no choice in the matter but when he entered through the back mother of pearl gates, Isadore blocked his way. He demanded, "Where is your harp? You were admonished to keep it with you and bring it back here!"

Greg's spirits sunk to a critical low but he apologetically answered, "I left my harp in Sam Klam's disco!"

Surprised!

My older brother Carl and I were driving around in his pretty little 1932 Plymouth convertible enjoying the scenery when all of a sudden a White Leghorn hen ran into the road. The frightened bird tried to fly out of the way but only managed to rise up to the level of the bumper and that was a fatal mistake. The impact threw the remains over a fence and down an embankment. I had seen a woman sitting on her porch just before the accident and when she put her paper down and started towards us I jumped out, hopped the fence and picked up the hen. The feathers came off easily so I pulled them all off quickly and hurried up to the car carrying the dead bird.

Carl had stammered out an explanation to stall for time but the woman was standing belligerently with her hands on her hips ready to confront me. "Well, Buster, what do you have to say for yourself?" she asked angrily as I stood there holding the bird by the head.

"Madame, we were so startled to see a naked hen run cross the road we just couldn't stop in time. However, if you have an ax I am willing to cut its head off so you can have chicken for supper."

She snatched it from my hand and started for her house mouthing bad words to us over her shoulder.

There is probably a moral to this story but none comes to my mind except perhaps "Step on the gas and get the heck out of here!"

Holding It All In

One of the most well-known comedians of radio and TV put on a performance in a small Vermont city. After going through his entire repertoire and working harder than he ever had, his audience didn't laugh or show the slightest smile. After knocking himself out for two hours, the entertainer was exhausted and welcomed the curtain coming down. He walked around among the people leaving the theater and finally overheard one old-timer say to his companion, "You know, that man was really funny. It was all I could do to keep from laughing."

Atlanta Airport

You gotta love this one even if you've never lived in the South. Southerners can be so polite!

Atlanta ATC: "Tower to Saudi Air 511. You are cleared to land eastbound on runway 9R.

Saudi Air: "Thank you Atlanta ATC. Acknowledge cleared to land on infidel's runway 9R. Allah be praised."

Atlanta ATC: "Tower to Iran Air 711. You are cleared to land westbound on runway 9R.

Iran Air: "Thank you Atlanta ATC. We are cleared to land on infidel's runway 9R. Allah is great."

Pause

Saudi Air: "Atlanta ATC. Atlanta ATC.

Atlanta ATC: "Go ahead Saudi Air 511."

Saudi Air: "You have cleared both our aircrafts for the same runway going in opposite directions. We are on a collision course. Instructions, please."

Atlanta ATC: "Well, bless your hearts. And praise Jesus. Y'all be careful now and tell Allah 'hey' for us."

What it took to get an 8th grade education in 1895...

Remember when grandparents and great-grandparents stated that they only had an 8th grade education? Well, check this out. Could any of us have passed the 8th grade in 1895?

This is the eighth-grade final exam from 1895 in Salina, Kansas, USA. It was taken from the original document on file at the Smokey Valley Genealogical Society and Library in Salina, and reprinted by the *Salina Journal*.

8th Grade Final Exam: Salina, KS – 1895

Grammar (Time, one hour)

1.   Give nine rules for the use of capital letters.

2.   Name the parts of speech and define those that have no modifications.

3.   Define verse, stanza and paragraph.

4.   What are the principal parts of a verb? Give principal parts of "lie," "play," and "run."

5.   Define case; illustrate each case.

6.   What is punctuation? Give rules for principal marks of punctuation.

7–10.   Write a composition of about 150 words and show therein that you understand the practical use of the rules of grammar.

Arithmetic (Time, 1 hour, 15 minutes)
Name and define the Fundamental Rules of Arithmetic.

A wagon box is 2 ft. deep, 10 feet long, and 3 feet wide. How many bushels of wheat will it hold?

If a load of wheat weighs 3,942 lbs., what is it worth at 50 cts./bushel, deducting 1,050 lbs. for tare?

District No. 33 has a valuation of $35,000. What is the necessary levy to carry on a school seven months at $50 per month, and have $104 for incidentals?

Find the cost of 6,720 lbs. coal at $6.00 per ton.

Find the interest of $512.60 for 8 months and 18 days at 7 percent.

What is the cost of 40 boards 12 inches wide and 16 ft. long at $20 per metre?

Find bank discount on $300 for 90 days (no grace) at 10 percent.

What is the cost of a square farm at $15 per acre, the distance of which is 640 rods?

Write a bank check, a promissory note, and a receipt.

U.S. History (Time, 45 minutes)

Give the epochs into which U.S. History is divided.

Give an account of the discovery of America by Columbus.

Relate the causes and results of the Revolutionary War.

Show the territorial growth of the United States.

Tell what you can of the history of Kansas.

Describe three of the most prominent battles of the Rebellion.

Who were the following: Morse, Whitney, Fulton, Bell, Lincoln, Penn, and Howe?

Name events connected with the following dates: 1607, 1620, 1800, 1849, 1865.

Orthography (Time, one hour)

[Do we even know what this is??]

What is meant by the following: alphabet, phonetic, orthography, etymology, syllabication?

What are elementary sounds? How classified?

What are the following, and give examples of each: trigraph, subvocals, diphthong, cognate letters, linguals?

Give four substitutes for caret "u." [HUH?]

Give two rules for spelling words with final "e." Name two exceptions under each rule.

Give two uses of silent letters in spelling. Illustrate each.

Define the following prefixes and use in connection with a word: bi, dis-mis, pre, semi, post, non, inter, mono, sup.

Mark diacritically and divide into syllables the following, and name the sign that indicates the sound: card, ba ll, me rcy, sir, odd, cell, rise, blood, fare, last.

Use the following correctly in sentences: cite, site, sight, fane, fain, feign, vane, vain, vein, raze, raise, rays.

Write 10 words frequently mispronounced and indicate pronunciation by use of diacritical marks and by syllabication.

Geography (Time, one hour)

What is climate? Upon what does climate depend?

How do you account for the extremes of climate in Kansas?

Of what use are rivers? Of what use is the ocean?

Describe the mountains of North America.

Name and describe the following: Monrovia, Odessa, Denver, Manitoba, Hecla, Yukon, St. Helena, Juan Fernandez, Aspinwall and Orinoco.

Name and locate the principal trade centers of the U.S.

Name all the republics of Europe and give the capital of each.

Why is the Atlantic Coast colder than the Pacific in the same latitude?

Describe the process by which the water of the ocean returns to the sources of rivers.

Describe the movements of the earth. Give the inclination of the earth.

Notice that the exam took FIVE HOURS to complete. This gives the saying, "He only had an 8th grade education" a whole new meaning, doesn't it?! Also shows you how poor our education system has become! And, NO! I don't have the answers. After this, who wants to go to the 9th grade anyway?!

Can you read these right the first time?

1) The bandage was wound around the wound.
2) The farm was used to produce produce.
3) The dump was so full that it had to refuse more refuse.
4) We must polish the Polish furniture.
5) He could lead if he would get the lead out.
6) The soldier decided to desert his dessert in the desert.
7) Since there is no time like the present, he thought it was time to present the present.
8) A bass was painted on the head of the bass drum.
9) When shot at, the dove dove into the bushes.
10) I did not object to the object.
11) The insurance was invalid for the invalid.
12) There was a row among the oarsmen about how to row.
13) They were too close to the door to close it.
14) The buck does funny things when the does are present.
15) A seamstress and a sewer fell down into a sewer line
16) To help with planting, the farmer taught his sow to sow.
17) The wind was too strong to wind the sail.
18) Upon seeing the tear in the painting, I shed a tear.
19) I had to subject the subject to a series of tests.
20) How can I intimate this to my most intimate friend?

Let's face it—English is a baffling language. There is no egg in eggplant, nor ham in hamburger; neither apple nor pine in pineapple. English muffins weren't invented in England or French fries in France. Sweetmeats are candies while sweetbreads, which aren't sweet, are meat. We take English for granted. But if we explore its paradoxes, we find that quicksand can work slowly, boxing rings are square and a guinea pig is neither from Guinea nor is it a pig.

And why is it that writers write but fingers don't fing, grocers don't groce and hammers don't ham? If the plural of tooth is teeth, why isn't the plural of booth, beeth?

One goose, 2 geese. So one moose, 2 meese? One index, 2 indices? Doesn't it seem crazy that you can make amends but not one amend?

If you have a bunch of odds and ends and get rid of all but one of them, what do you call it?

If teachers taught, why didn't preachers praught? If a vegetarian eats vegetables, what does a humanitarian eat?

Ship by truck and send cargo by ship?

Have noses that run and feet that smell?

How can a slim chance and a fat chance be the same, while a wise man and a wise guy are opposites? You have to marvel at the uniqueness of a language in which your house can burn up as it burns down, in which you fill in a form by filling it out, and in which an alarm goes off by going on.

English was invented by people, not computers, and it reflects the creativity of the human race, which, of course, is not a race at all. That is why, when the stars are out, they are visible, but when the lights are out, they are invisible.

An Intriguing Tale

In a mansion high above the Connecticut River lived a dysfunctional family of eight individuals. Mr. and Mrs. Abbey were elderly and depended on the rest of the household to take care of running the large estate, as well as managing their modest but secure investments. The couple lived in a spacious apartment on an upper floor overlooking the Connecticut River and the White Mountains of New Hampshire. Albert and Constance Bailey were the only other married people in the house and were trusted completely by the Abbeys. These two managed the business end of the place and saw to the needs of their employers, treating them with great kindness. The Bailey farm had been wiped out in the Great Flood of 1927, leaving the couple nearly destitute. Because they were good people and had lived honorable and productive lives, the Abbeys offered them employment and the security of having a home in the large house for the rest of their lives. It was a comfortable and enjoyable arrangement. Two spinster sisters and two bachelor brothers made up the rest of the clan and occupied several rooms on the lower floor.

Although the Abbeys and the Baileys set their table with a flair for formality, the rest of the family was excluded because of their atrocious table manners and loud talk. The proper upbringing provided them apparently was lost while they were away at a very liberal college where they partied and wasted time. They returned home with no plans for the future, perhaps just assuming the parents would always provide for them.

There was an air of surveillance among the siblings as if no one trusted any of the others. There were frequent arguments over trivial issues but chores were taken care of with little dissention. One of the women always did the shopping and errands. Two ancient cows were cared for by the oldest brother, while the other one cultivated a large garden that produced bountifully so the younger women canned and froze enough food for the household. Everything seemed quite secure, interest money came in to pay the taxes and other expenses but in truth all but the elderly Abbeys, of course, and the Baileys were making plans to gain control of the estate, not to share but to acquire each to his own. Many private plans were made clandestinely.

There seemed to be only two avenues for each sibling to seize the estate. One was to outlive the others one way or another and the second was to contrive some legal means to gain the estate. Not one of them had the intellect to pull off any kind of legal method and whoever outlived the others might be too old to enjoy the largess by the time the others had all passed on.

A large maroon sedan began to drive slowly past the mansion several times every day and on more than one occasion appeared to be taking photographs. No one seemed to know the meaning of this ominous intrusion and the suspicion increased considerably when the vehicle began a nocturnal patrol and was observed a few times to stop and turn off its lights. The older couples on the top floor became rather uneasy at this strange happening. Meanwhile the others began to experience periods of lethargy and a lack of interest in the daily routine. One or two of them felt quite ill at times.

The first casualty was the oldest sister. She died of pneumonia according to the attending physician. One of the brothers was next and it was determined he had eaten the wrong kind of mushroom.

Well, now. Let's see. Believe it or not I can't remember how this all ended! My memory fails me completely. So I guess it's up to you, my readers, to finish this story. I would really like to hear how it ends. You will each have a different way of ending this tale, I'm sure, and will have no one to blame----except Me. Perhaps the title of this book should have been, "Tales of Woe, and *Me*"

The End

To order additional copies of this and future books
by J. Francis Angier, visit

WWW.JFrancisAngier.com
Or
francisangier@comcast.net